Tales from the Shadow Clan

Hal Warfield

FOR ALL MY GIRLS

For Mimi, Lauren, and Olivia – my reasons for everything I do

CONTENTS

Introduction   pg

1   The Box of Tears   1

2   The Chamber Mountain   12

3   Fire Night   25

4   The Darkness without a Disguise   52

5   The Day of the Airborne Dreamers   74

6   The King of Circumstances   86

7   The Impatient Farmer   98

8   The Stillness Broken   104

INTRODUCTION

Shadow People are small, laughing beings dwelling in the boundaries between light and shadow. They are mischievous but not spiteful. Their chief love is to hear and tell stories. They whisper stories to you while you sleep and then listen to you dream. The sound of their voices is like the ringing of many small bells.

Whenever you stop suddenly - wondering if you've just heard someone calling you or a knock at the door or other faint sound - it's most likely the laughter of the Shadow Clan. Have you ever stopped while walking a familiar route - suddenly not remembering how you got there? The Shadow Clan have been playing one of their tricks. How about when you catch movement out of the corner of your eye - only to turn around and see nothing; yes, it's them . . . and those of us with ringing in the ears have been treated to a Shadow Clan sing along.

One of their favorite pastimes is fishing - but not the way you and I think. They use thin transparent strings; you've seen them, everyone has - they pass in front of your eyes in different shapes and sizes - only we call them floaters. Anyone who's tried to follow a floater knows it moves as you try to focus on it - the Shadow People love this trick.

You ask how big they are? They're very small - they've been mistaken for hummingbirds. You can sometimes see them glowing as eventide draws near in lengthening shadows when the smell of evergreen is in the air. They're distant cousins of the gremlins but smaller - they're more closely related to the sprites and the pixies.

What are their names, you ask? Oh, there's Ping and Ing and Pict and Gif and Dox and baby Tet.

If you've a moment, then, hear their stories . . .

Water Stories

1 THE BOX OF TEARS

In the land of Adara, a boy named Pietro lived with his grandmother. He loved to go for long walks among the hills that surrounded his home. One brilliant spring afternoon,  Pietro's wandering found him in a beautiful valley filled with trees and flowers - bright and fresh after winter's sleep. Breathing the sweet air deeply, he walked along, stopping now and again to listen to a bird sing or to smell a new flower. As he walked deeper into the valley, he heard the sounds of water merrily tinkling over rocks in a stream bed. Coming closer to the sound, he found himself in a grassy glade with a chuckling stream in the center.

The sun found holes in the leafy canopy overhead, brightly showing on the grass and sparkling in the water. Pietro was enchanted by the beauty of the place; he sat down on a warm smooth rock by the stream to rest.

As he looked out over the water, he noticed what he first thought was a small patch of fog hovering over the stream. As he looked closer, he saw that it looked more like a small cloud, and he wondered how a cloud could stay there without moving.

Suddenly, Pietro heard a voice speak out of the cloud! It startled him so he fell off the rock and into the stream! The voice in the cloud laughed; a sound like merrily ringing bells.

"You should be more careful, Pietro," laughed the voice, "you'd better get out the water now, you're scaring the fish."

Pietro stood up and stepped out of the stream. Water cascaded from his hair and his clothes. "Who are you, Cloud, and how do you know my name?" He sat down on the rock and took off his boots. Water poured out onto the grass.

"I am called Miasma, though my name used to be Ariatta, and I have watched you many times as you worked in your grandmother's garden and tended her goats and took walks among these hills." Miasma's form seemed to grow more compact, and her voice grew, it seemed, a little sad. "This glade has been my home now for many years. Except for the deer and rabbits and squirrels, I have had little company."

"But now that you have found your way here, I hope you will feel welcome to return and visit me." The voice brightened, "Of course, falling in the stream is entirely optional."

Pietro laughed despite being wet and a bit chilly. He was becoming accustomed to hearing a cloud speak though he was still very surprised - and curious.

"How can you have two names? And what do you mean that your name 'used to be' called Ariatta? Did someone change your name? And why should a cloud have a name anyway? And clouds shouldn't be able to talk, should they? Your voice sounds like a girl's voice; are you a girl?" Pietro finally ran down, his immediate questions exhausted.

Miasma floated in the air near Pietro. Her shape shifted as she spoke, and the sunlight made rainbow colors sparkle around her. "My goodness what a lot of questions! I don't know where to begin!

I was once a human girl named Ariatta and I lived in a land called Antaris. It is a beautiful place over the mountains far to the North. A mysterious stranger visited my home one day. He talked with my father and mother and told them of his journeys in many peculiar lands and among many extraordinary peoples. Much of what he said was in the form of riddles which my parents did not understand."

"I hid in an alcove outside the room where they visited and listened to the conversation. When my parents went to arrange for a meal to be served the stranger called to me, - "Ariatta, I know you are there; come out here, child."

"I came out hesitantly. The stranger smiled at me and said, 'You will have a wonderful life, Ariatta, but you must first experience the Box of Tears. Once you have spent time in the clouds, you will return to your mother and father and your home.'"

"And with this cryptic riddle, the stranger left our house and we never saw him again. I asked my parents what the "Box of Tears" was, but they were as puzzled as I, and even somewhat fearful. As I grew older, I always wondered what this strange saying meant but gradually it faded from my mind."

"One day when I was 12, I wandered high into the mountains looking for wild mushrooms to use in the special dinner mother and I were preparing for my father's birthday. On my way back with my apron full of delicate mushrooms, I tried to take a shortcut and came, instead, upon the opening of a large cave. I was drawn almost against my will inside and found that the walls glowed brightly. Soon I could no longer see the entrance where I had come in."

"What strange place was this? I knew I should probably run but I could not; I kept walking slowly but carefully over the rough broken ground. There was a feeling of great age in this cavern though I'm not sure how I knew this."

"Suddenly the cave opened out into a large room; a room that had the feel like that of the throne room in the King's castle. In the center of the room was a large square of polished rock about three feet tall. It gleamed with bright flashes of quartz in the dark rock, and it made me uneasy. I became even more uneasy when I saw a large wooden trunk sitting exactly in the middle of the raised rock surface."

"The trunk was carved with many figures and each figure was crying. Some of the carved people covered their eyes and others held their arms up in grief. They were all looking upwards toward something that was just out of sight - the carving did not show what they were looking at."

"I felt such a surge of sorrow and compassion for these sad people. I could not imagine what made them so sorrowful! Without thinking I reached out to touch the carved face of a woman whose hands were wrapped around her own body as if clutching a lost child. As I touched the box, the cave was filled with a rumbling sound that caused me to jump back in fear."

"The trunk slowly opened by itself. The lid opened fully, and I heard a voice, a familiar voice! It was all around me like a fog; above me and below me and around me and it was the voice of the stranger from so long ago."

"Ariatta." The voice sounded like the distant rumbling of thunder over the mountains. "You have entered the Great Hall of the King of Sorrows. He is king over all unhappiness and despair and pain."

"Who would be such a king?", I cried, "why would he not give up such an unhappy throne?"

The voice rumbled from a distance, "The King, my master, has an important calling. So important that without him the people of the world would soon be crushed under their load of despair. The King of Sorrows travels throughout the kingdoms of the world and gathers the tears of those who have sorrow and brings them here to be stored in the Box of Tears. As he gathers their tears, the peoples' sadness

becomes bearable and finally begins to fade."

"When someone loses a child or a husband or a wife or when a storm destroys

their crops, my master lessens their grief so that it can be borne and so that they can heal."

"But now over many years, the Box of Tears has become full. If not dealt with properly, the tears will spill out and bring new sorrow to all the peoples of the earth. Years ago, my master the King sent me out to find one who was pure of heart and merry in their soul to bear the contents of the Box of Tears and thereby keep the suffering and pain from returning to the earth."

Ariatta was afraid. "But why me? I'm not special. And I am sometimes sad myself."

The voice of the stranger drifted all around her. "You are sad, Ariatta, for others. For the child who falls and hurts herself, for the man who loses his business, for the animal caught in a trap. The King of Sorrows asks that you bear the burden of the Box of Tears for a time, and two times, and half a time, so that joy and happiness may continue among the people of the earth."

a time and two times and half a time

"What does this mean? How can I bear the tears of the world?" Ariatta slowly backed away from the Box of Tears hoping that the voice would leave her alone.

"If you agree, and you must agree of your own free will, you will join with the tears and together become a great cloud and your name will be Miasma - cloud of sorrows. If you agree, you will float over the earth providing rain and lightning and thunder. And over a time, and two times, and a half a time, you will become smaller and smaller until all the tears have returned to the earth as rain. When at last all the tears have returned to the earth, you will become Ariatta again and at that time you will begin a wonderful and happy life."

Miasma paused in her story and Pietro came to with a start. He had been entranced by the story the cloud had been telling. His clothes were almost dry, and the sun was beginning to grace the western sky. He knew he should be getting on home to his grandmother's, but he was spellbound by Miasma.

"You . . . you must have said 'yes' or I would not see you as I do now," Pietro said hesitantly.

Miasma's voice answered slowly, "You are right, I did say 'yes' to the voice of the stranger. I did not want to but something on the inside of me said it would be all right and my fear began to fade. I told the voice of the stranger that I would bear the Box of Tears if it meant that sorrow for others could be lessened."

"As I said this, the glow in the room brightened. The walls of the Great Hall were filled with sparks of glowing quartz, and I could see the water in the Box of Tears begin to bubble. A fog rose out of the box and engulfed me until I could not see anything but the mist. I cried out in fear because my very being began to fade and grow soft and began to merge with the mist rising out of the box.

"I felt myself join with the sorrows of uncounted people. I could no longer weep though because I was one with those tears and I, Ariatta, became Miasma. I billowed out of the cave and rose on the winds into the sky. In those early days I was a huge cloud bank carried over all the earth by the four winds. There were times when I was a soft gray blanket hiding the sun and there were times I grew into tall thunder heads full of rain and lightning and hail."

"Everywhere I drifted I brought rain to the earth. Sometimes I would fill a river where people fished. Sometimes I would moisten

fields where wheat grew. And, as often as I could, I would bring cool summer rains - rains that cooled the brow of the man working in the field and the woman tending her garden and the children who played in the rain with happy shrieks."

"So, you see me, my Pietro, after many years of raining and the world is happier because of this. But my time of service to the King of Sorrows is nearly complete and his promise of happiness is nearer day by day."

Her voice grew still, and her form began to expand. "Now I must return to the skies for a time. Please say you'll come and visit me again, Pietro."

"I will, most certainly I will, Miasma," said Pietro, "I'll return tomorrow after my work is finished."

Miasma rose into the late afternoon sky. Pietro's thoughts were filled with wonder and awe at a girl who had become a cloud and borne the sorrows of the world. He made his way back home in time for supper. He told his grandmother about his afternoon walk but he could not bring himself to tell her about the cloud that talked with him.

As often as he could, Pietro returned to the glade and talked with his friend; for that is what the cloud had become. He would sit enraptured as she told him of her journeys. Of people that lived on islands in the sea, of those who lived in the shadow of great mountains, and of those who rode wild horses across vast plains covered with green grasses.

He often thought he could see Miasma in the sky overhead as he worked in the fields and the garden. His visits continued through the fall and into the early winter as he endured the cold to visit his friend.

But the day came when the snow and ice did not allow him to make his way up into the hills. And he spent the cold dark months worrying that he would never see Miasma again. He tried to stay busy keeping his grandmother's house warm and cheerful, but he continued to be anxious about Miasma.

Finally, the sun of spring worked its' magic enough that spring itself was just out of sight around the next hill. A few spring flowers poked bravely up through the warming soil. Pietro hurriedly made his way up the hillsides with fear poking at his heart.

He arrived at the glade; the trees still bare of leaves and pieces of ice clinging to the sides of the stream. The only sound was the sound of the cold water as it rushed along.

Then, suddenly, he heard a faint voice, "Pietro, you came!" He turned and saw Miasma but she was dramatically changed! The cloud was hardly visible and seemed to have difficulty staying together.

"I waited for you through the long winter days and nights. I wanted to talk with you again." Miasma's voice grew weaker, "My time is nearly gone."

"No!" cried Pietro, "No, you can't go! You must not go, for I have fallen in love with you! All during these months I have longed to talk with you and now you tell me you must go?"

Even as he spoke, a ray of sunshine illumined the last wisps of cloud that had been Miasma. Pietro heard his name called but the sound of it faded as quickly as it had started.

He sat heavily on the same large rock where he had first met Miasma and he began to sob. His shoulders shook with his cries and his hands covered his face and his heart was filled with a great ache.

Suddenly he felt something touch his shoulder. It was a touch so light and delicate that he first thought he imagined it. He looked up and over his shoulder through tear-soaked eyes and saw the blurred outline of someone standing there.

"Shhh, Pietro, it is I, Ariatta. The King of Sorrows has kept his promise and I am myself again. And I, too, love you."

Rising quickly, Pietro grasped her arms. He saw a slender dark-haired girl with a serious face and merry eyes. Without knowing how, his heart knew that it was Ariatta.

The joy on their faces matched the bright glow of the spring sunshine as they left the glade arm in arm - knowing that their travels through life would be free of the cloud of sorrow.

And the Box of Tears remains . . . .

As they travel, Dox tells another story . . .

2 THE CHAMBER MOUNTAIN

Many years ago, before we knew that the Earth sails round the Sun (rather than the other way round), in the village of Si'moora, there lived a girl named Shuny. Shuny lived in a house made of wood and earth and covered overhead with the neatly tanned hides of goats.

Si'moora sat at the edge of a sparkling river which reflected the mountains beyond. On a calm day Shuny could see a perfect reflection of the snow-covered peaks of the Chamber Mountain.

Shuny and her best friend Vella would play at the rivers' edge; seeing who could make a flat rock skip the most times.

As they lay in the fresh green grass beneath a shady tree, Vella asked, "Why do they call it the Chamber Mountain?"

Shuny followed Vella's gaze out into the distance. "I don't think anyone knows why," answered Shuny. "My mamma doesn't know, and my father says it's just a name. When my grandmother was alive, she told me it was because the mountain was hollow!"

The girls giggled at the thought of hollow mountains. Vella sighed. "It's such a beautiful place." She and her family had come to Si'moora from another valley to the south two years ago.

One hot summer day, Shuny was walking along the river watching fishermen cast their nets from small boats. In the distance she could see the rainbow filled mists as the huge waterfall cascaded down the Chamber Mountain to form the river. It was a beautiful scene; one she had enjoyed throughout her 13 summers and one she took for granted that she would enjoy for the rest of her life.

The air was so clear that the sides of the Chamber Mountain seemed to be close enough to touch. Shuny shook her head and blinked her eyes. It seemed that she had seen a shimmer in the air that made the sides of the mountain seem to dance.

She looked again - something was happening! Then she saw that the fishermen had hauled in their nets and were rowing their boats for shore as fast as they were able. What was happening? In the distance she heard them shouting in fear. Then she saw it . . .

Far up the side of the mountain she saw a cloud of dust and rock. It seemed to move so slowly at first but even as she watched the cloud turned into a river - a river of rock! It was an avalanche, a rockslide moving swiftly down the side of the mountain, gaining speed by the moment.

Shuny was frozen like a statue. It seemed she was compelled to watch as huge boulders and unmeasurable amounts of rock slid down the mountain. Now the sound of the avalanche reached her; it was louder than ten thunderstorms. The ground itself seemed to roll beneath her feet causing her to almost fall.

The river of rock began to cover the ledges where the water spilled out to form the waterfall.

She finally found her feet and began to run toward the village. The avalanche continued as she ran, and the cloud of dust and rock obscured her sight of what was happening to the waterfall. Would this never stop?

Reaching the village, she ran through the narrow streets. Children were crying; adults were shouting and running in every direction. Sheep bleated in fear and tried to run, milling around their pens in waves of wool.

Shuny saw Vella and cried out to her. Vella turned and ran to Shuny, and they held each other tightly. Both of them were trembling and Vella had been crying. "Shuny, Shuny, what is happening? Is it the end of the world?"

Shuny tried to comfort Vella, "Shh, now, it will be over soon". And, as she spoke these words, she realized that it was true. The rock still fell but you could hear that it was not as loud. Over the next few minutes, the sound of the avalanche began to recede though the cloud of dust it created still filled the air.

Shouts could be heard coming from the rivers' edge. Shuny and Vella ran along with many other villagers to see what was happening. Everyone seemed to be pointing upriver toward the Chamber Mountain. Shuny called out to everyone, "What is it? What is happening?"

"The river, the river!!", called many voices at once. The girls wiggled their way through the crowd till they came to a place where they could see. The river was shrinking!

Off in the distance, the dust in the air was beginning to clear. "Shuny, look!", called Vella, "the waterfall - it's gone!" Sure enough the rocks from the avalanche had completely blocked the waterfall.

The people of Si'moora fell silent as the river shrank. The small fishing boats dropped with the water level and then came to ground as the water flowed away from them. More and more of the rocky riverbed became visible until all that was left of the wide clear river was scattered pools and rivulets. Some of the pools had fish swimming frantically around in circles.

Everyone was stunned. Some of the smaller children were wailing in fear. For a long time, no one moved. Then, almost at once, it seemed that everyone began talking and shouting and crying at once. For everyone realized that the river; the life of Si'moora was gone.

Fear walked through the village that night. A few people had already left for the long journey to the south and east where they had family. Shuny listened as her mother and Father talked in low voices about what to do. They had no relatives within walking distance; Si'moora had always been their home.

Shuny finally fell asleep from exhaustion, tossing and turning in her bed. When the light from the full moon shined in her window, Shuny began to dream. She was high up on a ledge of the  Chamber Mountain. A stooped figure walked toward her but somehow Shuny felt no fear. The figure came closer and spoke her name! Shuny recognized her grandmother's voice! But how could this be so?

"Shuny child," said the old voice, "Shuny, how you've grown!"

"Grandmother?" cried Shuny, "but you're . . . you're . . ."

"I passed away?" chuckled the little old women, "yes but anything is possible in dreams, child." Shuny hugged her grandmother joyfully, "But how did I come here? Why am I on the side of the mountain?"

"I've come to you, child, to tell you that you must be brave so that you can save Si'moora. I've come to show you how to open the Chambers again and release the great water within. For the mountain you see from home is a vast hollow cavern filled with the water of rain and snow.

But an ancient troll lives inside the chamber. He sleeps for a hundred years at a time and when he awakes, he is in a foul temper. When he awoke this time, he saw our peaceful village and anger filled his heart. With his thunderous voice and powerful strength, he caused the avalanche that blocked the waterfall."

Shuny asked, "what can be done, Grandmother? What am I against a troll?"

Her grandmother hugged her tight, "Hush, child, for I am here to tell you all you must know to take dominion over the troll. You must be brave and full of courage for I tell you that it is certain that you will succeed. I will show you an entrance to the chamber. In the morning you must slip away before your parents wake. Follow the path I will show you and enter the chamber. The Troll will hear you coming and challenge you. He is very ugly with large hairy ears and a loud voice, but you must show no fear."

"He will demand to know why you are there and threaten to roast you for his dinner. But he has a weakness - he loves word play and especially riddles! Tell him you challenge him to a contest of riddles. The first one to answer two riddles the other asks is the winner. If you lose you will indeed be his dinner. But if you win, he must return to sleep for 100 years after he opens new gates for the waters to flow again."

"But what are the riddles, grandmother? I'm not good at riddles," Shuny wailed. If I fail, I will be eaten. If I fail, I will never see my mother or father or Vella again. If I fail, Si'moora will be no more!"

Her grandmother looked at her and smiled, "Shh, child, do not look at the possibility of failure. You cannot fail for it is destined that you save your village. You will know the riddles to ask the Troll and you will be given the answers to his questions." As she spoke these words, she pointed to an opening in the rock wall above the ledge. "Here is where you will enter. Be strong, the Troll's defeat is sure if you face him bravely."

Her grandmother seemed to fade as she watched, and she cried out but her grandmother was gone and she had awakened in her own bed again. A faint brightening of the eastern sky told her that morning was near.

Shuny wondered at her dream, a troll? Her grandmother? It seemed like, well, like a dream in the bright sunlight. But that same sunlight shone on a village with no water and as the day went on more and more families left on the long trek to other villages.

"I must try," she thought, and she prepared for her journey. Taking some dried fruit and a small clay jar of precious water, Shuny started up the dry riverbank. As she walked, she thought about the troll and about riddles. The only ones she knew were simple and probably too obvious for the troll.

But as the mountain drew near, she began to have some ideas and by the time she started to climb the rocky path she was as ready as she could be.

The path looked unfamiliar until she came around a bend in the path and there was the ledge she had seen in her dream! She half expected her grandmother to be standing there waiting for her.

There was no one to be seen but there, ahead of her, was the opening she had seen in her dream. She thought that it might not be too late to turn around but the thoughts of her family and village spurred her on. With a bit of a tremble, she started into the passage. Light from outside shone ahead of her lessening the darkness.

As she progressed, she began to hear the sound of water splashing and in moments she stood at the edge of an enormous open pool filled with cold clean water! At that moment a deep snarling voice caused her to leap back in fear.

There before her stood a small broad figure; no taller than she but almost as broad as he was tall. His skin was as rough as the mountain rock and his face was dark with anger. On his craggy head he wore a crown covered in sparkling gemstones.

"Who dares to enter my kingdom?" his deep voice boomed angrily.

"I am Shuny from Si'moora, the village you have harmed by stopping our water. I have come to ask you to open the chambers again so that my family and the other villagers will have water to drink."

"The water in these chambers belongs to me," said the troll, "and your village and people are of no concern to me. In fact, your presence angers me; I have slept for 100 years and when I awaken, I find you have spoiled my splendid desolation with your village. I think I will eat you just for spite."

As he stepped towards her, Shuny remembered what her grandmother had told her - "do not look at the possibility of failure. You cannot fail for it is destined that you save your village."

"Eat me you may, King Troll, but after 100 years of sleep surely you would enjoy a game or a riddle or two? If I am a meal, you will soon be alone again with nothing to do." The troll's hairy ears twitched, and his red eyes gleamed.

"Riddles?" he said, "what do you know of riddles? You are a child and I have hundreds of years of practice with word play."

"Oh, well," said Shuny, "if you know so much, King Troll, then let us make a wager - whichever of us correctly answers two riddles will win the game. If you win, I suppose I'll become your meal but if I win you must open the doors of the Chamber Mountain and return the river to its' course." What she didn't say had to do with his returning to sleep with the loss of the wager.

The troll scraped his rough chin with his hand. Despite his roughness he loved word games. He knew that he could fool this child by hook or by crook so, after a moment, he agreed.

"Foolish girl, I will take that wager, win the contest and have you for dinner in the bargain. And since I am the king here, I will go first." And this was his riddle:

There's a word composed of three letters alone,

Which reads backwards and forwards the same.

It expresses the sentiments warm from the heart,

And to beauty lays principal claim.

Shuny shook inwardly. A three-letter word? Backwards and forwards the same? What did that mean - expressing heartfelt sentiments and beauty? She began to wonder if she should have come and if she could outrun this rough old troll.

"Give up? Already?" laughed the troll with an evil laugh. "The word that I seek is three letters long - and it's your EYE that expresses the sentiment of the heart and sees the beauty of the world - beauty that you will see for only a short time more."

"This will be a short contest indeed," gloated the troll as his evil laugh echoed across the water-filled chamber. "And since you failed the first riddle I will go again. Soon you will be my dinner."

The Troll chanted:

What is that which is -

The beginning of eternity,

The end of time and space,

The beginning of every end,

The end of every race?

Shuny knew that she must not fail this time; for herself and for her family and for her village. She thought deeply - what is the beginning of eternity? What is the end of time and of space? Wait! The end of every race . . . suddenly she *knew.*

"Oh, wise Troll, the answer is not in heaven or on earth but in our mouths - the beginning of eternity, the end of time and space and the beginning of the end of *you* is the LETTER "E"!"

The troll gnashed his teeth in rage and frustration. He howled in anger, "you answered that one rightly but my dinner still you'll be.

Since you answered correctly it is your turn to make a riddle but be warned, I have lived in this mountain for thousands of years and there isn't a riddle I haven't heard."

Shuny had considered this moment ever since her grandmother appeared in her dream. She took a deep breath and began to speak:

What can run but never walks,

has a mouth but never speaks,

has a head but never weeps,

has a bed but never sleeps?

The troll rolled his eyes and started to speak - then stopped with his mouth hanging open foolishly. Assorted rumblings came from his throat, but no words came forth. Shuny had him! She knew she had him!

"What no answer, King Troll? No idea that will save you? You will now return to sleep for 100 years and return what Si'moora so desperately needs. For that which runs and has a mouth and a head, and a bed is nothing less than our *RIVER* and now return us that which I have won."

The troll roared in anger and frustration and lunged forward to grab at Shuny. But in mid-lunge he was stopped. Amazingly, as he froze, he yawned - a huge gaping mouth-cracking yawn. And as he yawned Shuny heard a rumple from deep in the mountain.

"NO!" growled the troll, "No I have only wakened!" But even as he spoke his eyes glazed over and he stumbled backwards into the cave. As he fell Shuny heard the rumble grow into a roar. The rocks were moving! She turned and ran back down the rocky path, shrieking as lumps of rock as big as her head fell from the tunnel walls.

Behind her the snores of the troll continued to shake loose rock and as she gained the entrance to the cave, Shuny saw the walls of the Chamber Mountain crumble as unimaginable amounts of water sprang forth from the openings. Shuny stumbled and ran down the uneven pathway as she sought to avoid the rocks and water.

Finally, after what seemed an unending time, Shuny gained the relative quiet of the meadow at the base of the mountain. Turning to look she was overwhelmed by what she saw. A new series of waterfalls cascaded down the sides of the mountain filling the empty riverbed below.

She ran along the riverside laughing as the water began to form rivulets, then streamlets, which all combined into a torrent of fresh blue water white with bubbles and foam.

As she approached Si'moora, Shuny could hear the cheering of the towns people as they witnessed the return of the river. Boats began to float again, and flocks of water birds returned with the newly flowing river.

"Shuny, see," called Vella, "our river has returned! It's a miracle!"

And it was all that Shuny could do to resist saying, "yes, a miracle, until the troll wakes again!"

Fire Stories

The clan camped for the night near a country Inn. The Inn is hosting a family reunion of the MacShom family. Dox and Pict enter the Inn to see if anyone is telling any stories. They settle on the gleaming brass lamp stand where they are just two more twinkles in the brightly shining room.

3 FIRE NIGHT

The city lay sleeping in the moonlight.

No, literally, the city was asleep. But, you'll say, a city should be asleep in the moonlight. It's nighttime - the only ones who should be awake are the palace guards and a mother awake with a fussy child.

But you don't understand. The city was asleep in the moonlight, and in the daylight, and on a dark and stormy night. Everyone lay sleeping - the king with his crown over one ear, and the queen gently

snoring, all the guards slumped over where they had been standing. And in the city every mother and father and child

and butcher and baker and candlestick maker were fast asleep and had been for years.

How many years? No one knew for sure; and as I'm sure you've already figured out, the city of Fountinplay was under a spell. But it had been so long that no one outside the city could quite remember who cast the spell or why.

Had it been a spiteful troll angry from not being invited to the castle? Or a wicked witch envious of the beauty of the princess? Perhaps it had been the King of the Elves seeking to stop the growth of the city into the spaces of his kingdom. No, it may have been a devious Wizard who did it just because he could.

Be that as it may, the city of Fountainplay slept through the heat of summer and the cold of winter, through the leaves of autumn and the flowers of spring. And to make matters worse (if, come to think of it, matters could be worse) you couldn't even get into the city anymore to try and wake them up. In addition to the spell of sleep, a covey of dragons had moved into the area surrounding the city.

Question - do dragons come in a covey? Or is it a pod? I know it isn't a litter - that's puppies and kittens and these were no one's idea of pets. Oh, well, we'll leave it at a covey for now.

The dragons numbered in the dozens and dozens. They took to the sky at first light of day, flying and soaring and swooping and breathing fire the whole time. It was a dreadful sight and one which sensible folks used to scare the dickens out of their children when they were bad.

(Now, children, they would say, remember young master Hobbins. He was a bad child and now he is nowhere to be seen - the dragons seen to that! But, Pa, Yon Hobbins went to live with his aunt, didn't he? Now never you mind - the point is that dragons may come for bad children so mind yer manners and eat yer supper!)

Dragons, it seemed, had little practical use beyond this. Their swooping and their fire caused people to stay many leagues from their range; it was the sensible thing to do. But that left the people of Fountainplay to sleep on and on and on. Strangely, it was the dragons doing that finally started the process that lifted the spell. After all, nothing lasts forever . . .

On an especially hot August day, the dragons were wheeling through the sky, fighting, and snapping and breathing  fire. Two ill-tempered old males were fighting with tooth and claw and fang and flame when one snapped off part of the scaly wing of the other. This thick piece of wing fell into the city and crashed through the dome of the palace striking just in front of the king's throne! And even with this racket all in the throne room slept on unmindful of the noise.

But what did happen was this - a large ornate desk covered with gold and silver crashed over on its side and slid along the marble floor. This desk had been used by the King's Scribe who wrote down the words and decrees of the king. The top of the desk flew open and out poured a number of paper tubes which were coated inside and out with beeswax. These tubes had been used by the scribe to safely store the King's decrees.

With a clatter the tubes flew out of the fallen desk and rolled down the marble steps of the throne room. Striking the bottom of the stairs several the tubes continued rolling across the courtyard. Some of the tubes flipped sideways and caught fast. Others popped open, spreading the king's wit and wisdom across parts of the city. Picking up speed, the few remaining tubes began bouncing down the main street of the city. Past sleeping people and animals, more of the tubes burst open draping paper over bushes and barbers, hedges, and hogs.

Finally, one last tube escaped out the gate of the city and rolled down the hill on which the city was built. Rolling and bouncing, the tube finally took a great leap, flying end over end to land with a splash in the river at the bottom of the hill.

Bobbing in the current, the tube rushed along through the lands occupied by the dragons. On and on the river ran carrying the waxy tube with it. Finally, the river widened and slowed in its wanderings. The last tube holding the scribe's work came to rest on a muddy bank far from the city and the dragons.

Sometime later (did it matter if it was hours or days or months or years?) the riverbank where the brightly colored tube stuck out of the mud received visitors. The first indication was the sound of voices arguing loudly. Striding along the riverbank came a tall young man and struggling to keep up was a girl of nine or ten.

"Bozrell Stonewill, you slow down and wait for me!", the young girl commanded. "Stop right now or I'll . . . ."

"Or you'll what?", sneered back her brother, for Boz Stonewill was purposefully trying to irritate his sister - successfully it seems. "I'll kick you in the shins! Again!", replied Ovia Stonewill, "and this time you'll be lame!"

Stopping so suddenly that Ovia walked into her brother from behind, Boz looked down at his little sister with exasperation. Though they were ten years apart in age, you could see their family ties - each was dark of hair and complexion, with strong handsome features; now colored with irritation.

"All right," said Bozrell sarcastically, "I've slowed down. Now what?"

"You are always trying to leave me behind - and I think you enjoy it! I as little like traveling with you as you do me. But we are family and since mother and father died . . . ." Her voice trailed off and tears ran down her smudged cheeks.

Boz sighed. It had been a year since their parents had perished.

They were all each other had and they had been traveling now for over six months seeking a new place to live. Their travels had taken them through mountains and across plains as they sought a home and a means of making a living. Boz had worked anywhere and everywhere he could to keep them in food, clothes, and shelter. Ovia had learned to care for children younger than her while parents worked and, by doing so, contributed almost an equal share of their livelihood.

Kneeling and putting his arms around his sister, Boz sighed (he had sighed more in the last six months than in all the rest of his life) and hugged Ovia. "I'm sorry, little sister, I am hungry and tired and irritable. I'll try to be better. Now wipe your eyes and we'll stop here for a while and rest. I think yon stream would feel good on bare feet."

Ovia sniffed loudly and ran her rough sleeve over her face. "I'm sorry too, Boz, but I'll try to be more agreeable." Sitting down, she removed her battered boots and rolled up the legs of her pants. Boz settled down against a tree trunk and closed his eyes.

Parting the rushes at the edge of the steam bank, Ovia put one foot into the water. It was cold but it felt wonderful to tired feet. As she put the other foot in the water and turned to call out to her brother, an object in the mud caught her attention. Was it a tree branch? No, it was too smooth. Leaning down she grasped and pulled with all her strength. It moved but would not come out of the mud.

She called to Boz, "Help me - I need your help." Boz stirred and swatted a fly off his nose, "Not now, dirty face, I'm still resting."

Summoning her mother's stubbornness, Ovia yelled, "Help me NOW - I've found something!" That got Bozrells' attention.

Joining his sister on the mud bank, Boz grasped the tube and pulled hard. With a sticky sound the tube came free. He climbed back on the bank looking at the smooth cylinder with puzzlement. Ovia was soon looking over his shoulder as he examined the tube.

And as often happens when faced with a puzzle, he began guessing what it might be. "Is it a spy glass? Or maybe someone's' travel pack? It isn't very heavy." he said, giving it a shake. He might have continued this if Ovia hadn't grabbed it from him.

Pulling on one end, she said, "The best way to find out it to open it", and she continued to pull at one end and then the other. With a soft pop, the lid flew off and sheets of fine parchment paper slipped out.

"Now you've done it," yelled Boz, reaching for the tube. Paper continued to roll out onto the grass and the breeze began to spread the paper in all directions. For a few moments, Boz and Ovia danced around each other, first grabbing at paper, then bumping into each other, then shouting directions to each other, finally ending up in an exhausted heap on the grass with all the sheets of paper in hand.

Boz finally looked up and said, "You couldn't wait a moment, could you? I would have gotten it open sooner or later."

"At the rate you were going it would have been much later, brother." Ovia began looking at the papers in her hands. The parchment was the color of fine linen and soft to the touch. It was covered in script done in a fine hand; smooth and flowing.

"The King of Fountainplay decrees that all ducks, no, duchesses must wear less jewelry than the queen," read Ovia. "Fountainplay? I wonder where that is. And whose papers are these?"

Boz was reading a page of his own, "'The King of Fountainplay sets forth this day a decree that the all the people must bring a day's produce of their farms and shops and mills as tribute to the King's birthday.' Ovia, these are the papers of a king written down by someone in his service. But how did they get here?"

Puzzling over their find, the brother and sister continued to read; even after they continued on their way Ovia continued to read which caused her to stumble several times.

As evening approached Boz and Ovia approached a small-town gleaming in the late afternoon sun. As they had so many times before, they began looking for a place to stay and perhaps someone who would share a meal with them. During their travels they had slept in barns and in the open under the stars and in a cave and, a few times, in the homes of friendly folk who took them in.

The town was called Nypara according to the sign at the outskirts of the city. Boz kept his eyes open for someplace he might work and earn some badly needed coins. As they approached the town square, Ovia began to look for mothers with small children who looked like they could use help.

Seated at the well in the center of the square was an old blind man. He worked with nimble hands at a small loom before him. In some amazing way he wove a cloak of many different colors even though he could not

32

see his work.

Boz and Ovia sat a small distance from the man who looked in their direction with uncanny accuracy. Ovia felt uncomfortable under this blind gaze. "Good evening to you, children," said the old man in a low rumbly voice. Though surprised, Boz answered with respect, "and good evening to you, sir, but . . .".

Semml laughed (for this was his name) and said, "How did I know you? At the very edges of things there are no boundaries. As you walked by, I sensed you, as you sat down, I heard you, as you looked at me, I saw you."

This seemed to offer no opportunity for reply, so they remained silent. Semml continued, "You have traveled far and are weary. Is there something an old man can do to help you?"

Boz spoke again, "Kind sir, we look for a place to sleep and the opportunity to work to earn our living. I have experience in many occupations and my sister is skilled at taking care of children."

The old man turned his attention to Ovia, "So, young one, you are grown beyond your years and all this travel and travail because of the loss of your parents. Yet your future seems bright; it glows around you in the evening light."

"Sir, you are blind; how do you know these things?", asked Ovia. "My eyes no longer receive light but eyes that do not see do not make one blind. It is the attitude of the heart that says whether one sees or not. I see beyond what eyes can see - and I perceive that you are tired and hungry (That, thought Ovia, was an easy guess). Come with me to my home and I will share what I have with you."

Packing his loom in an old sack, Semml rose to his feet and, with the aid of a long stick, began walking. With a bit of apprehension, the they followed a distance behind the old man.

Semml quickly got ahead of them and turned a corner. As they hurried to catch up, they turned the same corner only to find that they had lost the blind man. How could that be? They had only been a few steps behind. Walking slowly now, Boz and Ovia looked here and there, through open doors and windows. And just when they wondered if he had been a figment, the old man's voice came from behind them. Boz fought to seem calm, but Ovia jumped straight up.

The old man stood in an open door beckoning to them, "This way children, remember one doesn't see with eyes alone." Entering the low door, the children came into a small, neat room. Everything had a place, and the room was full of color; bright shards of glass suspended by strings made a colorful pattern in the setting sunlight. Rocks and crystals filled odd spaces in the walls and glowed in purples and reds.

At a small table at the back of the room, Semml had placed loaves of hard bread and cheese, a pitcher of goat's milk, and a basket of fruit. "Come children, eat and rest yourselves and tell me of your journey."

Hunger overcame their lingering caution and soon the three were eating and talking. Semml looked from one to the other of the children as they spoke, still seemingly able to see them in some strange way. When their story approached the events of earlier in the day, Semml for the first time seemed surprised. "Papers in a tube? A colored tube full of papers with writing? How did you come upon this, children?"

His voice had risen in excitement and Ovia saw color come into his cheek. "I found the tube sticking out of the mud of a stream bank. Boz wouldn't help me at first but then he finally came and helped me pull it out of the mud. Then we both pulled at it until the end of the tube burst open and all these papers fell out and then we read them, and they are from a city called Fountainplay . . . "

Semml sat up with a start, which frightened Ovia and stopped her torrent of words. "Fountainplay," said Semml in an odd voice; so odd that Ovia pushed her chair back from the table and even Boz shifted nervously in his chair.

"Fountainplay was my home as a child; Fountainplay is from where I fled when I was very small; and Fountainplay is where I am exiled from today. Fountainplay is the ever-sleeping city with none to wake them and Fountainplay is home to dragons."

The old man fell silent then and an air of sadness filled the room. For several long moments no one spoke until Ovia reached out a hand to touch the old man's arm, "Please, sir, don't be sad. I don't understand what you mean about a sleeping city. Please, sir, tell us what you mean."

But Semml shook his head. Straightening he looked at his young guests, "Not tonight, child, not tonight. For the hour is late and you need rest." Startled, Bozrell realized that later afternoon had turned into night as they had eaten and talked.

"Behind that door is a room where I store my weaving materials. You will find cloth and yarn that will make a comfortable bed. Rest now and let sleep knit the 'raveled sleeve of care'." With that the old man retreated to another small room to sleep.

"Well, that was more than odd," thought Boz as he prepared to sleep. Ovia had fallen asleep as quickly as her head had hit her makeshift pillow of yarn and cloth. Laying down with his head on his pack, Boz wondered what the old man meant when he called Fountainplay a city asleep and as he fell asleep a soft glow seemed to emanate from the paper tube.

The bright light of morning found its way through a crack in the wall and onto Ovia's closed eyes. Dancing dust motes made colorful speckles as she slowly opened her eyes and, as she had done so many times before, wondered where she was.

Familiar snoring told her that her brother was still asleep and bright yarn on the floor in front of her reminded her of their strange host.

Sleeping city . . . dragons . . . exile . . . Standing quietly, she entered the main room of the house and quickly realized that no one else was there. On the table where they had supped were pears and bread and the juice of grapes. But Semml and his loom were gone.

Stopping only to eat a bite, Ovia entered the now busy street. Merchants and maids, goats, and goatherds - the city bustled with sight and sound. Retracing her steps from the night before, Ovia soon heard the splashing of the fountain where women came to draw water. She was looking for children to care for, but she was also looking for the old blind man.

As she drew near the fountain, she spied Semml in his place weaving his colorful trade. She came near him to offer him good morning when he looked up and said, "Well, little one, you are here early. Have you had your breakfast and where is your brother?"

Astounded, Ovia stopped with her mouth open. "How, where, who", she sputtered. For the market was noisy and she had said nothing. With a smile the old man beckoned her to sit with him. She sat and watched as lambs and small children took their place for water.

Semml continued his story from the previous night as if he had just paused to take a breath. "Fountainplay lies many leagues to the north from here. My mother and my father lived on a small farm on the lands

 just outside the city wall. My father raised sheep and my mother used the wool to make soft yarn. We also raised grapes and berries and with these my mother colored the yarn.

The city rose above us on the hill, and I loved to see the bright banners on the city walls waving in the wind.

On feast days we would sometimes travel into the city to see the king and queen as they rode by in a carriage pulled by proud black stallions. The King and Queen would ride to the gates of the city as all the people cheered and then they would ride back to the steps of the palace where the King would speak stirring words to the crowd.

I was too young to know exactly what he was saying but my mother would say that the King was a proud man, and my father would hush her. I was also too young to understand the talk later that day as we stopped to visit my mother's sister. My uncle spoke of dragons that had been seen in the distance by travelers. My father said that there had always been dragons somewhere or other, but my uncle interrupted him, 'these dragons are much closer to Fountainplay than ever before - and no one seems to know why they approach. What if they come even closer?'

A shadow passed over our celebration and no one spoke of it anymore, but I knew my mother was worried. We returned home and went about our days as we always had - Father tending the vines and the sheep. Mother tending house and creating beautiful woven cloth for sale.

Some days later I heard shouting along the road before our house. A group of people was hurrying along down the long hill from the city. They made me afraid because they were afraid. Children cried and fathers yelled, and mothers and grandmothers pleaded for them to go faster.

My father tried to speak to those hurrying by but was ignored. Suddenly my aunt and uncle appeared out of the crowd and almost fell into our house. "We must flee, we must hurry,' said my uncle, 'The dragons are almost upon the city - something happened in Fountainplay and now we must flee!'"

Ovia realized she had hardly been breathing and stopped to shake her head - Semml had stopped speaking, gazing into an unseen distance. "What . . . what happened then?" she asked; almost afraid to hear the answer.

Looking at her with unseeing eyes, Semml continued, "My father and mother rushed to gather a few belongings so we could flee. As we started down the road towards the others a dark shadow came over the sun, growing larger and larger. My mother screamed and my father urged us to hurry; he turned to face the dragon whose shadow covered us. I cried out and tried to run but my mother held me tightly. The flame that stole my father from me also stole my sight. When the heat and stench finally passed my father, and my sight, were both gone."

"My mother and I wept as we fled, seeking a hiding place. We crept into a small wet hole in the hillside where we waited, miserable and sad, for night to fall. For dragons do not fly at night but sleep where they land."

"So, by day we hid as the dragons wheeled and fought overhead and by night we fled further and further from Fountainplay. At last, we arrived here where my mother raised me and took care of me until she passed away many years ago. As I grew, I began to perceive many things around me. I could see the brightness of people though I could not see them directly. I could hear the undercurrent of their thoughts. And that is why, small one, I said that your brightness glows."

He paused in thought, "The dragon's breath stole my eyesight but gave me an inner sight that now serves me. But in Fountainplay no one sees - all dream in endless sleep."

Ovia started as from a dream, "But what caused the sleep? Why do the dragons rule over the city? What is to be done? They must be saved, yes?"

"If they are to be woken, we must first discover why they sleep. This evening we will read the words of the king in the papers you found and perhaps there we will find the answer."

The day waxed and waned and before long it was evening. Boz had worked with a craftsman that day and had earned wages. He had bought bread and cheese for supper. After they had eaten the old man stirred the fire to brightness. "Now, children, let us hear the king's papers read."

Ovia opened the tube and pulled out all the papers. Much of what was there was everyday business concerning roads and buildings and crimes and punishments. But the final pages held more interest: "The King has decreed that the Dragonsbane flowers are reserved for the enjoyment of the royal family. The possession of these flowers by any but the royals will result in imprisonment."

Semml stirred, "The Dragonsbane are bright, fragrant flowers - they grew wild all over the city. They king must have grown jealous of their beauty - read on."

Ovia looked at the next page, "The shortage of Dragonsbane makes this necessary . . . very few flowers remain and are therefore reserved for the king and his family."

The next page was written in a more hurried and less neat hand: "All citizens of Fountainplay must flee for the last Dragonsbane has died and dragons are seen throughout the kingdom. I, Contil, scribe to the King write these last words. Dragons wheel through the sky overhead; their foul breath is affecting everyone. The king and queen are unconscious, and others are falling where they stand. Have mercy on Fountainplay - the pride of our king and the loss of our Dragonsbane have doomed us all. We will sleep forever. Now I must end this record though no one will ever see it." And just below these words were scrawled,

"The seeds of day from dragons drop, at night must be stolen - a promise to keep.

The teeth of the dragon are seeds that are granted, for flowers to bloom and rid us of sleep."

And there the writing ended. Unseen, Bozrell had joined them as the last words were read. "What is this Dragonsbane that is spoken of?" Ovia jumped at his voice; she had been lost in a vision of dragons wheeling through a dark sky.

40

Semml spoke, "Dragonsbane is a bright flower that grew wild throughout the kingdom. Its' bright hues and sweet scent were part of our daily lives. I was only a child then; I did not know that the flowers were dying."

His unseeing eyes sought those of the children, "Will you help me? Will you help me find the way to waken the sleeping people of my land?

Bozrell's eyes widened in alarm, "no, I will not take my sister in the way of harm. You ask too much, old man. I . . . I am sorry that your people are sleeping but my sister is my only family now and I must protect her."

Ovia whirled on her brother, "how can we not help, Boz? All we have done for these many months is walk from place to place and I am tired of it. Why should we wander with no purpose through life?"

"But, Ovia, we do not know what we will encounter on the way and then we must pass through the land of dragons. It is simply too dangerous. And without the flowers how will anyone awaken? I do not even know the way."

The old man's voice interrupted them, "but I do know the way and will lead you safely."

"Lead us! Safely! You are blind, old man, how can you think you can lead us. How can the blind lead the seeing?"

Semml paused and then replied, "Am I blind? Thanks to the dragons, I see more than most and often more than I care to see. I will travel with you and show you the way. I will not slow you down nor be a burden in any way."

Boz looked at the old man and then at his sister and then at the sky, "Fine, we have little future as it is - we may as well face dragons. Lead us, old man."

The next morning the three left Nypara on the highland road

41

leading north into the hills. Semml walked with a stick but had no problems on the rough path.

After they had traveled in silence for several hours, Ovia finally spoke, "Semml, how will we wake Fountainplay? Where do we find Dragonbane? He didn't speak for several moments, and Ovia thought he hadn't heard. Then, suddenly, he repeated the verse,

"*The seeds of day from dragons drop, at night must be stolen - a promise to keep.*

The teeth of the dragon are seeds that are granted, for flowers to bloom and rid us of sleep."

"The answer lies herein - the legends my mother told me as a child say that Fountainplay is built on the old breeding grounds of the dragons. Dragons live for hundreds of years but throughout their lives they continually lose their teeth. According to the verse, these teeth are the seeds that blossom into Dragonsbane. As the town grew the flowers began to die off and when the last faded so did the city."

Boz, who had been scanning the way before them, now turned, "Dragons' teeth? Dragon's TEETH? Are we on a fool's mission then? Why did you not tell us this before?"

Semml looked at him with uncanny, unseeing eyes. "I did not say it would be an easy task but one that would require courage. I have a way and a plan that I will tell you of when the dragons appear."

Dubious and furious, Bozrell was tempted to leave the old man and return the way they had come with only his sister. At that moment, that option disappeared.

A shadow covered the sun followed in rapid succession by two more. Wheeling above them were three scaly, smoke-belching dragons sizing them up from on high.

"Run," cried Semml as he turned toward a rock outcrop at the top of the next hill. As they ran, the dragons retracted their wings and stooped like a hawk or an eagle. The three ran for their lives though Boz

and Ovia saw no hope for them. As they reached the rocks, Boz thought that their lives were forfeit but looking up in amazement he saw first Semml then Ovia vanish before his eyes.

The first dragon hurled a stream of fire from open jaws and Bozrell felt the tremendous heat on his backside. Just as the flame reached out for him, Boz fell headfirst into an opening in the rocks. Rolling forward his nose caught the awful stench, and his eyes streamed with tears from the deadly fumes. But the worst of the heat passed over them and the other dragons wheeled back into the sky with cries of confusion and rage.

Boz lay completely still for several minutes - he was afraid that the dragons would land and come for him. Finally, he looked up and around and then ahead into the shallow cave; for that was what he had fallen into. Wiping burning eyes, he strained until he made out two shapes before; the larger one must be Semml and the smaller one was Ovia.

His sister ran to hug him tight, crying to herself with fear and relief.

Rolling to sit up, Bozrell simply sat for more long moments, holding his sister tightly. "Oh, Bozrell," his sister sobbed, "I thought you were dead."

Finally beginning to recover, Boz shook his head, "I cannot leave you, dirty face, I promised to take care of you." Looking at Semml, Boz asked, "How did you know this was here?"

"I was not sure, but I remembered how rocks such as these often hid small caves where I played as a child. Now children we are committed. We must wait here till night falls before we move forward. Dragons sleep soundly at night, and we may pass among them.

As the shadows lengthened and evening approached, the three stayed still in the shallow opening. Overhead they heard the shrieking cries of dragons as they came to roost on the burned fields ahead. Semml faced the brother and sister. "Now listen carefully and I will tell you what we must do . . ."

Now darkness was complete and only a few stars glimmered in the night sky. Creeping out from their hiding place they looked towards the north. In the distance they could make out the beginnings of the mountains wherein lie the sleeping city.

"We will be as quiet as mice now," said Semml. "The dragons will sleep from dusk till dawn, and we will find our way among them. My sight is gone yet still I will perceive the dragons and lead us around them. As we travel through the sleeping ones, we must feel the ground as we go. The teeth of dragons are curved and rough like stones. As you feel them with your fingers, pick them up and place them in your travel bags. Long before dawn we will have found our way through them and our way to Fountainplay will be clear."

Boz and Ovia strained to see. As their eyes adjusted to the dark, they could see only enough to keep from falling headlong. As they moved forward across the blasted field it seemed that large rocks covered the plain. But suddenly one of these rocks snorted and shot a small jet of flame from its nostrils. The dreaming dragon illuminated the fact that each rock was a sleeping dragon!

It was at this moment that Ovia's courage failed. Hearing tales of dragons and seeing tails of dragons were two completely different things! The momentary burst of flame had ruined their night vision. Ovia stood in fear, trembling, and thinking her heart would give them away by its pounding.

She knew that in a moment panic would cause her to run and in running she would expose them, but she could not help herself. It was at that moment that strong arms enfolded her and held her in a safe firm grasp. Her brother had dropped to one knee: sensing her terror. He could not even whisper to her, but his strength flowed to her and stopped her panic.

As the moment passed, she realized that she could see again; if only faintly. Her eyes had readjusted to the faint starlight. Calmer now, she and Boz followed the old man as he led them on a circuitous path through the sleeping monsters.

Silently now they moved and with each step they let their fingers brush the ground. At times they felt rough rocks and the thorns of briars. But every few moments their fingers made out the rough shape of a dragon's tooth. Picking these up, over and over, they made their way forward. But Ovia had discovered something else about dragons - they smelled BAD. The odor that hung in the air was foul; like old burning garbage that had sat in the sun too long.

Her eyes watered and stung, and she stifled several sneezes that threatened to expose them again. She slowed a bit to rub her eyes and nose. Ahead of her she could just make out the shapes of her brother and Semml as they moved left around a large sleeping shape. As she moved to catch up, she missed a small shape ahead of her; missed seeing it but did not miss stepping on something. Something that was at the same time hard and pliable.

A soft cry arose from the shape - she had just stepped on the tail of a baby dragon! This baby was the size of a horse cart and its skin had not yet produced hard, leathery scales. The baby was more startled than angry as it whirled around to face Ovia. Stepping around the baby dragon, Ovia tried to move toward her brother. But now the baby was more curious and followed her. "Wheep?", it said, "wheeple?"

"No, baby," Ovia said, "no, go back, don't follow me." She continued backing away from the baby dragon that now followed her as

she went. Now the baby dragon raised its head and cried out in frustration and with that cry everything changed. With a snort one of the large sleeping rocks came suddenly awake as it looked about for her baby. The mother dragon could not see well in the darkness but heard the plaintive cries from her baby.

Lighting off a burst of flame, the dragon whirled to see Ovia standing frozen in the fading flame light. Then a voice rose in loud command - "RUN!"

Semml no more than uttered the word then he turned to the north and began running. Even as he ran, he continued to reach down and grab fallen teeth. Now other dragons were coming awake from the commotion. Spouts of flame and angry growls arose as the confused dragons tried to see what was happening. The night erupted in fire.

Ovia and Boz followed the old man as he ran. Boz followed the old man's example and continued to gather teeth as he ran but Ovia could do no more than run. They wove among the now agitated dragons that were still uncertain what was happening. Flame lit the night sky often enough now that it was like running through a lightning storm. Running, dodging, falling - they ran for what seemed an eternity.

Now the dragons seemed to sense their direction and the flames came closer. But dragons cannot fly at night, so their flames mostly struck the burnt field or other dragons that screamed in anger and pain. Each moment seemed to be their last and when it seemed that they could run no more the first light of dawn appeared to their right, lightening the sky.

With the dawn's early light, the dragons began to stretch their wings and prepare to take to the sky. The three reached the beginnings of an old upward path that headed up the mountain.

"We are within a few miles now," the old man wheezed, "when we cross the first pass, we can begin to plant the seeds we have gathered. Keep running."

As the dawn grew in strength the dragons wheeled into the sky. They pursued the three with gouts of flame and heat, which drove them into every small hiding place they could discover.

Ahead Ovia saw the ruined gate opening in a ruined wall. The outer limit of the city was upon them. Looking up and straining to see as the sun washed the sides of the mountain, Ovia could see the shape of the sleeping city in the distance.

The three stopped for a moment under an overhanging rock. Exhaustion was written on each face, but the old blind man encouraged them, "We may now begin planting the seeds of dragons' bane. Each tooth must be completely covered with soil; the darkness and cool moist dirt will cause them to bloom quickly."

Gathering themselves they began the race up the hill. Every few moments, Ovia felt in her bag, grabbed a seed, and thrust it into the soil beneath her feet. Dragons swooped and screamed in anger shooting rivers of flame and heat down on them. Each moment she feared she would fall and be consumed in a blast of heat. But each moment she zigged when the dragons zagged and so made her way up the hillside.

Bozrell reached the inner wall of the city and was amazed when he fell over a sleeping guardsman who had dropped where he stood. The falling probably saved his life as a dragon shot flames where he had just been standing.

Shaken, he crawled forward planting dragon's teeth as he went. He had long since stopped wondering if there was any hope; it seemed that this would be his last effort.

Rising to his feet, Boz looked ahead to see Semml and Ovia several hundred feet ahead among the houses and buildings of the city. He staggered forward in a poor attempt at a run. Overhead a large old male dragon took sight at Ovia moving more slowly now through weariness. Folding his wings, the dragon stooped much as a hawk or a kite does at their prey. As he approached faster now, Ovia became aware of the rapidly expanding shadow. She turned and faced the dragon unable to run any more.

With a scream of triumph, the dragon spewed a river of flame toward the child. At the moment of her oblivion, Ovia was struck by a hurtling shape, which shielded her from the heat and blast.

Bozrell had gathered all his remaining strength and had run up the hill toward his sister. As the flame raced towards her, Bozrell leaped knocking her sister aside and at the same time feeling a searing pain across his neck and shoulder as the flame struck him.

Now Ovia dragged her injured brother, moving him against the wall of a building. A few feet away, the old blind man continued putting dragon's teeth beneath the soil. Overhead the old dragon saw the three sitting unmoving. Settling to the earth the dragon moved ominously toward the exhausted trio.

Semml looked at the brother and sister, "Thank you, children, for your effort. I am sorry that we failed. But I believe the city will rise again." The old dragon approached closer and eyed them with malice. Raising his head, the old male roared at the sky in preparation of covering them with flame.

But at the moment of of their doom a small movement at her feet caught Ovia's final attention. Out of the ground burst a shoot of green and a flaming flower of red. The sweet odor burst from first this flower than another and another and other. Rearing back the old dragon screamed in frustration now.

The odor of Dragonsbane began to fill the air now as first dozens,

then hundreds, and then thousands of bright flowers blossomed. With cries of rage and pain, the dragons wheeled into the skies, rising on powerful wings seeking to avoid the pungent flowers.

And now, around the three, the flowers aroma spreads like a soothing blanket. Though exhausted, Semml, Ovia and Bozrell mounted the steep street toward the palace. As they walked, they heard the murmuring of many voices now awakened for the first time in - well, does it matter how long?

Finally, they mount the steps of the castle itself. Entering the royal chamber, the three stand before the king and queen as the light of morning greets their opening eyes.

It is now many years later. It is a great feast day in Fountainplay; Dragonsbane abounds in bright violet and orange and blue and red. Banners wave from every high tower. The people throng the streets dressed in bright new finery, making their way up the steep streets to the castle courtyard. There is singing and the playing of instruments and jugglers and magicians and street players and all manner of excitement.

Just then the sound of trumpets fills the air with clear, bright notes that seem to rise up into the air. The voluntary rings out, bringing cheers from the throats of all the people. Up the main street comes a parade of soldiers dressed in gleaming armor and carrying spears with tips that catch the sun like points of fire. Behind them come mounted horsemen; their steeds dressed in the finest of colors as they carry helmeted soldiers.

All the people strain to see what is next - then they pick up cheering again. Riding on white stallions come Prince Bozrell and Princess Alcina. The bridles of their horses were festooned with Dragonsbane; the bright flowers flowing down like water. It is the marriage day for the prince and princess - they mount the hill and enter into the courtyard of the palace. Coming behind them on a stallion black as midnight rides Contessa Ovia Dragonbane; one of the saviors of the city. As she enters the courtyard she looks upward to the entrance to the great hall.

Her eyes seek a special place, a place of honor at the right hand of the king's throne. Seated on a seat that could almost be called a throne in itself sits an old man. He is a man with blind eyes who sits seeing all this is unseen.

And the happiness in Fountainplay is that of those who wake from sleep to the light of a bright new day.

May we all aspire to live in the brightness of day

4 THE DARKNESS WITHOUT A DISGUISE

The people of Liol lived at the edge of Great Darkness. It had not always been that way. Most of the people in the town could remember when Darkness was far off to the north and never came near Liol. There were other villages - Moro and Ibicol and Geaze - which now lay abandoned, covered in Darkness.

Over the years the Great Darkness had slid slowly South softly like a dark bank of fog. To stay in Darkness meant disaster as those foolish enough to try quickly discovered. "I will best the Darkness," someone would say - and it was always the last thing anyone heard from them.

So gradually, over time, entire towns and villages moved Southward, staying ahead of Darkness. As they arrived in Liol, one frightened family posted this strange warning on a sign by the Northbound Road:

Only the most unwise enter Darkness without a disguise.

And now as the Great Darkness approached Liol, the people were both angry and frightened. "When will this stop," they would say, "must the whole world be covered by Darkness? And what happens to those who try to stay in Darkness? We look for light, but all is darkness; for brightness, but we walk in deep shadows. Something must be done!"

Great wizards and warlocks would travel to the edge of darkness and recite dark and awful curses against Darkness. But like a deep cave, Darkness would swallow up their words without as much as an echo.

One of those who came to Liol was Dub. Dub was a journeyman wizard 2nd class. This meant that he had only recently finished his apprenticeship with a master wizard. With sandy hair that had the tendency to stick out in spikes and a round happy face, Dub did not inspire much awe or respect. In fact, he was often mistaken for a porter or even a farmer. This was a little embarrassing for Dub but mostly he didn't mind.

He came to Liol by happenstance. He was on his way to Miller Pond to visit his master and teacher and to take a post-graduate class in medicinal funguses.

As he approached Liol, the bright sun was high above, and Darkness was only visible if you knew where to look for it. Dub sat by the side of the road and leaned against a signpost to rest. As his head tilted back to rest on the post, he became aware of the sign atop the post. He tried reading it upside down, but it came out "Squeezing Winter Silliness with Union Soup" which didn't make a whole lot of sense.

So, Dub leaned farther and farther to the right until his head and body were almost on the ground. "Darness?", he mumbled, "what is Darness and why is it Disgusting?" Puzzled now, he finally stood up and read the sign in its fully upright position.

This only made him feel slightly embarrassed and even more puzzled. "What is Darkness and why do you have to dress up to go there?", he wondered. After scratching his head several times which only served to make his hair stick out in further in every direction, Dub decided to continue on into Liol. Night was still hours away, but he wanted to learn more about this darkness.

If there was night, you might be wondering, then what was the difference between night and darkness? The night still followed the day, but Darkness knew no hour, nor breakfast time, nor mid-day tea, nor afternoon, nor sunset. No friendly stars twinkled through Darkness, no round ruddy moon could be seen through Darkness.

Darkness absorbed the day and ignored the night and those who had no fear of night still dreaded darkness.

Dub entered the village and stopped before the Inn of the Singing Frogs. A trio of frogs carved from a wooden plank announced that there were beds and meals to be had within. Entering the Inn, Dub sidled up to the bar and listened quietly to the conversation around him.

"They say that Darkness is all of the bad things that people have done," said one, "and the bad deeds are finally coming back to haunt us."

"No," said another, "Darkness is another world that is trying to take over our world - it is filled with ghouls and demons and trolls which is why no one ever comes back. Darkness captures them forever."

"I saw Addy Simpton go into Darkness last winter," said an old man in tattered clothes. "Darkness was at the edge of my farm then - I had a family and a home and livestock. Addy said that Darkness was nothing to fear and told me that he would prove it." The room grew quiet. Though it was obvious the story was not new, it still got everyone's attention.

The old man continued, "I watched him walk toward the Darkness at noontime. He was a big strong man who feared nothing, so his stride was quick and confident. But as he approached the Darkness, the Darkness approached him! It seemed to reach out an arm and sweep him toward the foggy gloom. He faded into the Darkness like a shadow crosses the moon at night.

As he vanished, I saw him turn to me with fear on his face. His mouth was open as if he was shouting at me, but I heard no sound -

Darkness captured even his final words. He was driven from light into darkness and is banished from the world."

The inn was as silent as if Darkness had swallowed up all of their words. The old man sighed, "my family has gone further south towards Neemon, but I stayed to watch over my animals. Now they are all gone - taken by Darkness."

Dub realized that his mouth was hanging open and quickly closed it. His first thought was that he should beat a hasty retreat from Liol, putting as much distance as he could between himself and Darkness. As he left the pub, intent on heading south as quickly as possible, another thought occurred to him.

"What if I could sneak into that Darkness . . . maybe bring out something that proved I'd been there. These folks would think I'm a hero." But as often happens it would be fate, not planning, that brought Dub and Darkness face to face.

Dub hurried along with his thoughts racing alongside him until he arrived at Miller Pond. There he approached the crooked old house of his Teacher - the Master Wizard Ooligoth. Dub rang the bell and waited. And waited. And then waited some more.

Just when he thought that he had gotten the days wrong, a deep slow voice came through the door. "Who is that ringing at my door? I want no visitors today - visitors may come on the first and third day of the week only! Now, go away!"

Dub thought about doing just that (he was always a bit afraid of Ooligoth) but summoning some courage he called out, "Teacher, it is I, Dub the Apprentice. We had an appointment to study fungus, remember?"

"Dub the Fungus?", replied his teacher, "I know no one named Fungus."

"No, master, I am Dub. I was your student; I have returned at your calling." Dub was beginning to feel that he'd have a better chance finding Darkness than getting through to his teacher.

The door to house creaked open halfway and a tall dark shadow seemed to issue forth. With a suspicious eye, Ooligoth looked Dub up and down and then sideways. "Oh, so it's YOU, is it? Weren't you supposed to be here next week?" questioned the wizard. "I don't seem to remember an appointment now."

Finally thinking he'd have to sleep in the town square under the open sky, Dub tried one more time, "Teacher, I have traveled many leagues to return to your house. I have braved the open road and the open sky to get here. I have even come close to the land of deepest night, of deep shadow and disorder, where even the light is like Darkness."

At the mention of Darkness, Ooligoth actually stepped out of the doorway and into the street. He loomed over Dub and with an even deeper voice said, "Darkness? What, boy, do you know of Darkness? Get in here now and don't keep me and the funguses waiting any longer."

With a slight feeling of dread, Dub passed over the threshold of the wizard's house. He followed the old man's shadow through familiar rooms and passageways until he came before his old room. Here he had lived for two years as an apprentice and, evidently, here he would be again for a time.

"Rest now, Apprentice Dub, for an hour or so and then we will proceed with your training. I've got to find that bag of mushrooms - I remember seeing them here somewhere." And with a few more mumbles about funguses, Ooligoth vanished into the maze that was his house.

That evening as they shared a meal, Dub told Ooligoth of his journey and of his encounter with the people of Liol. He spoke hesitantly and almost apologetically about Darkness; he did not want his master to think him foolish.

Flickers of firelight caused deep shadows on the old Wizard's face and smoke curled in strange patterns from the pipe held in his hand. Ooligoth's words were slow, and Dub had to lean forward to catch them, "Only the most unwise enter Darkness without a disguise". The words seemed to entwine themselves with the smoke in the air.

Dub sat back with a start, which also startled the old cat sleeping on the hearth. "Why that is what the sign said outside Liol, Master, what does it mean?" The Wizard's eyes gleamed in the firelight, "The Darkness is the work of a thief and a magician named Neg'loom. He is a thief because he stole a gem of power from me many years ago and he is a magician because he turned the power of the gem toward evil and darkness".

"Neg'loom came to me years before you, Dub, and, if the truth be known, he wormed his way into my confidence through my pride. He praised me and fawned over me, and my pride grew with each false compliment. I began to teach him my runes and spells and potions in the mistaken notion that Neg'loom would use them for good as I had."

Ooligoth stopped and the silence grew in the darkness until Dub thought his old master had fallen asleep. As he reached out to touch the old man on the wrist, the Wizard started which caused both Dub *and* the cat to jump this time.

With the warmth of anger stirring in his voice, Ooligoth continued.

"Neg'loom began to turn my spells and runes around and inside out - where I meant a blessing, he spoke a curse. Children were sickened and water turned sour, and crops did not grow. Suffering grew throughout the region, but I was too blinded by my pride to see the trouble and pain he was causing."

"When the townspeople came to me to plead for mercy, I finally began to see that my pride had come before my fall, and great would that fall be!" In anger I sought Neg'loom in his room and throughout my house but, knowing his time was short, he had fled North from Miller Pond towards Liol. And much to my increasing anger and shame, I found that he had stolen my most powerful of gems - a huge, gleaming pearl of great price."

His voice, which had risen nearly to a shout now dropped off to a sad whisper. "This beautiful pearl gave whoever owned it the power of multiplication and magnification. If you blessed someone that blessing was multiplied. If the people lived in fear, you had only to speak "Peace!" and peace would cause the fear to leave.

I pursued Neg'loom league after league, but his lead was too great for me. I cried out for him to return the pearl of great price he had stolen. But Neg'loom had evil in his heart and when he had traveled to a lonely place in the north, he brought forth the gleaming pearl from its hiding place and gazed deeply into its center."

"I am Neg'loom - master of the pearl and of its' powers. In my anger and hatred of all things I now steal the light from the lands of men. I curse the light and, in its' place, speak DARKNESS!"

"As he howled these words, I was still a league or more off yet, even at that distance, I saw the gleaming pearl change in a twinkling from pure, bright white to an inky blackness that absorbed the light around it. The Darkness swirled around Neg'loom who howled in evil glee. The Darkness began to grow and expand and suck the light from the sky. I was driven back and could not stand against the darkness. As I fled the

Darkness continued to grow and has continued to this day."

The Wizard paused and the final flashes of the fire on the hearth showed great sorrow on the old man's face. "Everyone who goes into darkness is ensnared by it. Whole families and villages are frozen in Darkness; unable to flee, unable to move, but most horribly aware and conscious of their fate. I have tried on many occasions to return; to rescue the pearl but the power of darkness is too great for me. The only recourse is in the rune repeated in writing and in speech, 'Only the most unwise enter Darkness without a Disguise'."

"There is a way to approach Neg'loom and free the pearl, returning it to light by stealth and cunning. But without the right disguise, the one who tries will be captured and held just as all the rest."

In great weariness and sadness Ooligoth rose and turning to Dub, he spoke, "So now you know of Darkness and of my pride and of my fall and of the pain and suffering I've caused. I will leave you now, but rest will not come for me." And with those words he left the room.

Later Dub was in his room as well and rest would not come for him; in fact, the hair kept standing up on the back of his neck each time heard a board creak or wind whistle in the kitchen chimney. He thought of all the people captured by Darkness and then thought about the people of Liol who would soon be captured if they did not flee.

It was not until a few hours before dawn that Dub finally dropped into a troubled sleep. He heard evil laughter as he tried to run from the approaching Darkness. But he could not run; his legs were like lead weights. Just when Darkness reached out to grasp him, Dub woke up. He was trembling and covered in a cold sweat. The nightmare had seemed so real!

This was the moment that something changed in Dub, emotions welled up in his soul - anger, fear, determination. He had no idea how, but he would find an answer to free those trapped in darkness.

Somehow, he slept again and dreamed again. This dream was markedly different from the first. In this dream Dub saw a man dressed for battle wearing a bright, plumed helm and carrying a lance. At the

head of the slender lance was a bright crystal point that gleamed with an inner light. As the warrior approached Darkness it fell back like black fog from the light of the crystal. Try as he might, Dub could not see who the warrior was and the gleam from the crystal lance head hurt his eyes. He reached up to shade his eyes and stepped back. His feet flew out from under him . . . and he awoke to find himself face down on the floor with the sheet wrapped around his ankles.

"Wonderful," he thought with disgust, "A warrior is what is needed to defeat Darkness and I cannot stay successfully in bed." With many a snort and sigh of frustration, Dub managed to dress himself for the day's activities.

But his mind wandered as Ooligoth droned on about moss wort and bell fungus and how a certain mushroom could cure the vapors. He daydreamed about striding with confidence into Darkness, of overcoming Neg'loom, of freeing the captives, and, with a blush, of winning the heart of a fair maid.

It was now lunch time, but Dub could not eat. While Ooligoth mumbled his way to the kitchen, Dub went into the yard behind the house. Here were the beehives that supplied Ooligoth with honey and a large old shed that Dub had climbed during his apprenticeship. His mood was grim with overtones of helplessness - How could he overcome Darkness. And yet he remembered his resolve the night before and in the depth of his feeling he reached up with his fist and swung it against the wall of the old shed.

Well, this action had unexpected results. The first results could have been predicted. Dub howled in pain and grabbed his now throbbing hand with his good one. This was accompanied by an impromptu dance of pain around and around in a circle.

The unexpected results could be seen as the door of the shed creaked open spreading a cloud of dust and age. Dub stopped hopping up and down on one foot as he realized that he had never seen the inside of this shed.

Though his hand stilled pained him, his curiosity throbbed more than his hand. What was stored here? He didn't remember Ooligoth ever referring to it. He had sat on the roof as a young boy and thrown crab apples at the goats in the next field, but he had never thought to look inside.

Peering in, Dub could see only shadows at first but as his eyes adjusted, he saw old trunks and cases stacked as high as the roof line. Musty old smells assaulted his nose, and he stubbed a toe to go along with his injured hand. Lifting the lid of an old chest he saw many rolled parchments covered in runes. Rummaging among them he realized that there was a large object in the bottom under the rolls. Reaching in he pulled the heavy thing out and saw that it was a tarnished old helmet.

With a start, Dub realized he had the beginnings of his disguise! It wasn't the beautiful helm of his dream, but it would cover up his spikey hair. As he rose and turned to leave, the top of the chest fell shut pushing it back into a corner. Something stored in the corner fell forward and added a lump on the head to his injured toe and hurt hand.

Muttering a few choice bad words under his breath, Dub grabbed the offending item and threw it out the door before him. Taking the old helmet, he walked out of the shed and back into the sunlight. The item that had thunked him in the head was an old javelin; a long smooth shaft with a dark smooth head attached with thick leather.

Dub's eyes lit up. Here was the other piece of his disguise. He now had a spear and a helmet and, looking down, he saw that there was another parchment inside the helmet. Pulling it out, Dub sat down and unfolded it. The writing was smudged but Dub finally made out:

Only the most unwise enter Darkness without a disguise.

With helm and lance by his side, the wise man seeks a pearl of great price.

Then, those trapped in Darkness dread hand, will see a great light . . .

This was puzzling and exciting at the same time. Here was a rune and a riddle concerning Darkness! What did it mean? Who was this hero? Dub finally realized that it didn't really matter. If he was to follow through with his plan, he would have to figure it out as he went.

Hiding the lance and helmet behind the shed, Dub returned to the house. He spent the rest of the day pretending that nothing out of the ordinary had happened. This pretending took the form of loud whistling whenever Ooligoth looked at him.

After a half-hearted attempt to eat his evening meal, Dub continued his acting by producing numerous large yawns. Finally, he excused himself and went to his room.

From there it was a matter of waiting till Ooligoth made his way to his chamber; then Dub sprang into action. The springing only got him as far as the door which took this occasion to squeak loudly. Freezing in the passageway, Dub could hardly breathe as he waited for Ooligoth to come storming from his room, but it didn't happen.

Making his way into the yard, Dub retrieved the lance and helmet. He had already tucked the parchment with the runes into his pocket. The night was clear, and a full moon shown in the sky lighting the roadway before him. He headed back up the road towards Liol and with each step his courage waned. "What a foolish thing to do," he told himself, but something within drove him forward. He encouraged himself with thoughts of freeing the people trapped in Darkness.

So wrapped up in this train of thought was he that it was a complete surprise when the moon winked out suddenly and the night became very dark indeed. There in the middle distance before him was the edge of Darkness. And this was not the friendly darkness of the clear, moonlit night. This Darkness was deep and inky and textured, and it writhed like a dense living fog.

At this point Dub almost panicked. At this point his courage almost failed. At this point he almost turned and ran. At this point fate stepped in to give Dub a push into his destiny. Turning to run for his life, Dub took only long enough to slap the helmet on his head and grab the lance. His first step, however, ran his bruised toe directly into a rock sending pain shooting through his foot. The pain sent Dub reeling straight backwards and, with a shock, straight into the edge of Darkness!

The world vanished before him, but he hurt too much to realize it yet. His next misstep was to hook the end of the lance on a branch of a tree which whirled him around the other way. This was one spin too many for him and the next thing he knew he was sitting on the ground with the helmet over one eye and the lance across his knees.

It took several minutes for the ringing in his ears and the throbbing in his foot to even think about subsiding. As they finally did it began to dawn on him that his situation had gone from bad to worse. It was as dark as the inside of a sack at midnight. He could not see the proverbial hand in front of his face and with a jolt Dub realized he was in Darkness.

His heart hammered in his chest as he looked this way and that way but could see nothing. He dropped his head into his hands and began to weep. Fortunately for Dub and for those trapped in Darkness the weeping did not last long. For one thing he realized that he was not frozen or trapped. He could move, he could stand up, which he did. He used the lance to steady himself and discovered something else.

There was a bright glow emanating from the long-pointed head of the lance. And at that point in his adventure even a faint glimmer was

enough to give him hope. By the light of the spear, he realized that he could see about him just a bit. He reached up to remove the helmet and quickly found that to be a dreadful mistake.

With the helmet removed, cold gripped him to his core. Not the cold of winter but the cold of deepest darkness. He stiffened and found it more difficult to move by the moment. With a desperate spasm of his muscles, he managed to place the helmet again on his head. Instantly the coldness and stiffness subsided, and he could move again. This turn of events necessitated a few minutes seated on the ground shaking like a leaf.

But then he realized that the helmet had saved him from the fate of others who had been trapped in darkness. It might not be much of a disguise, but it seemed to be working! Dragging himself upright again he held the lance above his head. Either the light was brighter, or his eyes had adjusted for he could now see several feet around him. The land was frozen but not with frost or snow. Nothing moved, there was no sound and the Darkness was very, very complete.

As he turned this way and that seeking a direction to escape the Darkness, Dub noticed that in one direction the light brightened slightly. Like a compass needle pointing north, the sharp point of the lance seemed to point to some strange north of its own. He didn't know what else to do so with a deep sigh Dub set off in the direction where the lance was brightest.

Darkness meanwhile seemed to try to enfold him, to stop him, to fasten his feet to the ground. It was in this frightening moment that Dub got his next shock. Something appeared in the light of the lance. Something? Or someone? With a gasp of disbelief Dub came across a family frozen in flight. A large man carried a baby girl and held the hand of a woman who must be his wife. Her hand was frozen to the hand of a young boy behind her. They had been running; seeking escape from Darkness when it overtook them and froze them in place.

Holding the lance closer, Dub realized in horror that their eyes were still alive. They could not move but they lived! He reached out to take hold of the man's arm, but he might as well have tried to move a tree trunk. The eyes of the man pleaded with Dub to help them but there was nothing he could do.

He spoke. "I do not know how but I will free you from your prison - but take hope, I will not fail you." And with that he looked again to see where the lance shone the brightest for now he knew that the lance was not leading him out of Darkness but deeper into the deepest Dark.

As he walked now, he thought desperately about how he could find the pearl of great price. So deep was his thinking that he almost walked into the next group of captives. A small cart pulled by a pony was frozen in time. The driver was an old man leaning forward to urge the pony on. Seated next to him on the seat of the cart was a young maiden. Dub thought he had frozen again himself; so beautiful was she that the breath caught in his throat. Her hair was flaxen and caught in ringlets around her face. She was looking forward as if she saw salvation with her arm upraised and her hand pointing the way to light and freedom!

But Darkness had stolen the freedom from her at the last moment. Even now Darkness seemed to try and cover her and clutch at her and keep her from being seen. Dub's heart was lost in an instant but as his heart was lost, his determination to free her and the others grew into a mighty white-hot surge of emotion throughout his being and into his very soul.

As he stood there, he found that he was no longer afraid. The people trapped in Darkness *would* see light again. Dub stood tall now and raised the lance aloft. In response the light brightened in *that* direction. With a final look at the old man and the beautiful maiden, Dub set off again. Avoiding groves of trees and piles of dark rock and frozen groups of people, Dub made his way deeper into Darkness.

But now a sound reached his ears. The sound was faint but even at this distance it sent shivers up his spine. As he moved towards the sound, the light from the lance seemed to dim but in reality, it was a small fire up ahead that made more light than the lance. Peering around a rock Dub saw a fearful sight.

Around this fire danced a wild-haired figure; it was none other than Neg'loom the black wizard. The fire burned fitfully but in its light Dub could see a circle of people frozen in positions that seemed to indicate great pain. But no one moved or made a sound. Only the light from the fire gleaming in their eyes showed that they were alive. Alive and suffering.

But worst of all, floating above the fire's light was a gleaming black orb. It twisted and spun and sent off great waves of darkness in all directions. As it spun, Neg'loom sang:

King of Darkness and King of Pain,

I hold my subjects in thrall.

Darkness deeper than any night

hides the light - from souls appalled.

Those who serve me ring my throne,

frozen but living are they.

The world will be mine in darkness sublime,

and none will again see the day.

Many thoughts ran through Dub's mind as he watched. Part of him was afraid again. But a larger part was remembering the people of Liol and Miller Pond who would soon be consumed by Darkness. He thought of the villagers in the pub, he thought of Ooligoth his teacher. But most of all he thought of the beautiful maiden frozen in unrelenting torment in the darkness.

He knew he must do something and tried to formulate a plan. He would creep as close to Neg'loom as he could and then rush him with the lance, knock him to the ground and then grab the pearl and run; escaping till he could figure out how to return it from dark to light.

Well, by this time we all should know that Dub's plan didn't work out quite like he hoped it would. Creeping out from behind the rock, Dub began moving the last yards between himself and Neg'loom. But immediately the black wizard whirled around and held Dub in his gaze and upraised hand.

"Soooo," the voice hissed, "you think to steal my dark orb? To lift my Darkness? Not so easy a task, my young fool. All my captives I have held in sway; do you not think I cannot hold you too?"

Dub felt cold and fear along his arms moving into his chest. He gasped for air as the black wizard struggled to hold and freeze him.

In desperation Dub gathered all that was left of his strength and determination and with a cry charged forward with the lance held in both hands. As he ran the light from the lance began to pulsate and throb casting great hideous shadows among the captive throng. But as he came within a few yards of Neg'loom - Dub did that for which Dub was now somewhat famous. His toe, his already bruised and battered toe, smacked into a rock on the path and, with a howl of pain, he threw both hands forward as he fell. The helmet flew off his head and the freezing effect of Darkness began to grip his body.

The lance took off like a bolt from a crossbow. Neg'loom threw up his hands to ward off the needle-sharp point, but the lance did not strike Neg'loom. Flying free, light now pulsing from the tip, the lance flew straight and true directly into the center of the pearl!

An explosion of light greeted the impact of lance and pearl, streams of lightning and showers of sparks flew off in every direction. Neg'loom

gave a great cry of despair and leaped for the pearl but at that moment the effect of the lance defeated the Darkness of the pearl and bright rays of dazzling light shot from the pearl in every direction. The cry of despair became a scream of agony as the black wizard was engulfed in the streams of light. Everywhere the light touched him began to smoke and with a final twist of pain and agony the author of Darkness exploded!

Darkness began to flee from the light - the light from the pearl shown in the Darkness and the Darkness could not withstand it. Wind like a hurricane swirled round and round the ring of frozen souls and the light from the pearl reached out even to the sky above. With a final pulse of light, the pearl dropped to the ground as the glorious sunshine poured in.

As the light of the sun found its way back to the earth that light touched each person like a warm loving hand. The people who had been frozen in Darkness had seen a great light and the light freed them from their prison and torture.

Each man and woman and child began to stretch and cry and reach eager hands up to the sun above as it drove the pain  from their bodies. They began to dance about and hug each other or sit on the ground in amazement.

But what of Dub? In the joyous confusion of the moment, Dub was nowhere to be seen. The people began to look around for their savior. They drew back to see Dub seated on the ground rubbing his oft-injured toe and looking somewhat dazed. The people set up a cheering and shouting that added to Dub's discomfort. He had only defeated

Darkness through clumsiness. How could he face them?

The freed population of Darkness knew nothing of this - they ran to him holding out their hands to bless him or kiss his hand. Silently Dub walked through the crowd, stopping to pick up his helmet and the lance that had saved them. He then stood over the pearl and realized what a great price had been paid. Leaning down he grasped the now glowing orb and held it above.

"People once trapped in Darkness," he called out in a loud voice, "if it be asked of you how your salvation came about today then say this - the people who walked in Darkness have seen a great light and the glory of the orb has saved them. It was not by might or by skill or by wisdom you were saved this day but by grace and the light from above."

With those words Dub placed the pearl in his pack and turned to go. But someone in the crowd called out, "Long live the Man of the Lance who conquered Darkness!"

And the crowd picked up the cry as they hoisted him to their shoulders. "Long live Lance! Long live Lance!" Carrying him so they began the trek back toward the towns they had left. More and more people joined them until the mass of people could be heard for many miles. As they approached the former edge of Darkness, they let him down from their shoulders. Ahead the people of Liol had run to see what had happened. Fathers and Mothers ran forward to hold the children they had lost. Brothers separated by Darkness reunited. Husbands and wives held each other tight.

In the confusion, Dub stood off to the side. He started as a hand touched his arm. He turned to see the beautiful maiden with the flaxen curls standing next to him. "Good Sir," she said in a soft voice, "to whom do I owe my gratitude for freeing my father and me?"

Her eyes sought his and they were the color of the summer sky. "Er, ah, well, my name is Du . . " He stopped. He thought. He smiled, "Fair lady, I am called Lance".

72

The hero business is an exciting one but for Lance he had had enough of being a hero. Today in Liol you'll find an apothecary and part-time wizard living with his wife and children. And each day as the sun begins to set in the West, Lance removes a cloth of velvet from a stand and on that stand is a softly glowing pearl of great price. And all who see it remember that Light is stronger than Darkness.

Air Stories

Dox is certain this story is true. He says his father told him this story when he was just a bright spark in the early summer evening.

5 THE DAY OF THE AIRBORNE DREAMER

He was born on the day of the Airborne Dreamers. Everyone in the village agreed that this was a favorable omen through no one was sure just exactly what it meant. He was filled with visions from an early age, and he had the power or the ability to make those dreams come true. He was very sensitive to the thoughts and needs and hopes of others and he had the ability to share his dreams with them.

Jontu was his name and, while he wasn't a great talker, the results of his efforts were plain to see. As he grew, he became the Wizard

Jontu; though this was mostly just a nickname. Jontu worked to see what was invisible. He couldn't accept what was obvious for all to see without studying it for that which was not seen.

He dreamed of flying and loved to sing and dance - if the singing and dancing were out of earshot of the villagers. Jontu was too shy to do these things in public. As he grew to be an adult, he maintained the face and nature of a child. His feelings were like a deep lake hidden beneath the earth. It took much work to reach this lake but the depth and richness that was there would take your breath away.

Jontu lived on a hill a short walk from the village. He was generous to all who came to see him, telling them stories, giving them freshly baked bread, and listening to their troubles. Anyone who came by his house inevitably left with a lighter heart.

One day Jontu had walked far into the woods following the will-o-wisp till he came to a clearing amongst the trees. The day was so beautiful and the sun so warm that Jontu felt compelled to sing.

"At this moment, someone is flying, right now, they soar through the air," he sang. Birds and squirrels paused in their daily routine to see who this was. Oh, they thought, it's just Jontu, and they went back to their tasks.

At that moment Jontu was startled as he heard a voice singing along with his. The voice was soft and gentle and floated to his ears on the breeze. *"Just now, someone is seeking, searching for someone who cares,"* sang the voice. Jontu looked around with astonishment, not frightened but curious.

"Who are you? And what are you?" Jontu asked. He looked about but could see no one. He looked up at the trees, but the birds could not help him.

The voice laughed. "I am Norii, Jontu, and we cannot see each other. You cannot see me because I am a sprite; a being of no material substance, and I cannot see you because a sprite cannot see at all.

Jontu was beginning to be confused. "If you cannot see me then how do you know me? If I cannot see you then how am I hearing you?"

The voice that was Norii came now from behind him. "Oh, Jontu, you ask many questions. Are you always this curious? A sprite is a being of light and vibration and energy. I can use this energy to make waves in the air. Waves in the air are what you call sound. So, you can hear me. If I made different vibrations, you would perceive me differently. Now watch."

Jontu looked around. Now in front of him he began to see sparkles of color in the air. It was as if fireflies had developed the ability to flash in blue, red, yellow, pink, and orange. Jontu was enchanted.

The lovely sparkles faded and Norii spoke again. "That is not easy, Jontu, and it tires me."

Jontu was chagrined. "I am sorry, Norii, I didn't know. What can I do to make it up to you?" Her laughter filled the air again. "Nothing, Jontu, just be my friend is all I ask. There are not many of us and even a solid like yourself is welcome company."

Jontu was uncertain whether he had been insulted or not. "A solid? You call me a solid? What does that mean? I'm a person!"

"I'm a person, too," Norii responded. "Being solid just means that you have substance; that you are made of flesh and blood. But being solid does not make someone a person. A person is someone who lives, and dreams, and experiences life and I can assure you that I, too, am a person."

The sound of Norii's voice grew fainter. "I must go and rest now, my solid friend, but I will come to visit you again."

"When?" Jontu almost shouted, "when?" He was not sure how, but he knew that this sprite had already become very important to him, and he did not want to lose her.

"I will come to visit you when you would not be expecting visitors." And with that, the voice faded away.

His mind was as troubled as the surface of the sea during a storm. Jontu could think of nothing else. He had trouble sleeping and his homemade bread developed a scorched place on the bottom crust. This was unheard of and the people in his village wondered at it. Some of the older women nodded their heads sagely as only wise old women can.

"Jontu has met someone," said one. "A girl perhaps?" said another. "But who could it be?" said a third. No one was unkind because they all cared for Jontu.

The next evening was the evening of the full moon. Jontu was very tired from his lack of sleep, and he nodded off in the big chair by the fire just as the full moon rose above the treetops. As he slumbered, he began to dream. It was his favorite dream - the one where he could fly through the air like a bird.

As he began to fly, his first thought was - "there's my house" - and then he was amongst the clouds. Jontu had just executed a perfect swan dive off a cloud when he heard his name being called.

"Jontuuuuu," called the voice, "wait for me." He was astonished and forgot to fly and fell straight down for several moments before he caught himself.

Out of the moonlight flew a . . a

It was a beautiful girl! Hey now, this was a really good dream! The girl in his dream flew up to and alongside him laughing with delight. "So, Jontu, you decided to join me in my world."

Jontu was astonished! The voice belonged to Norii! For the second time in his dream, Jontu forgot he was flying and made a really lovely dip and recovery as he overcame his astonishment.

"But, but, but . . .", he repeated foolishly, "How, how how . . ."

Norii laughed and swooped in a big circle, "I caught you speechless, Jontu! I told you I would come to you when you least expected me. Well, here I am! Catch me if you can!"

Norii and Jontu flew through the night sky, chasing and laughing. Rounding a cloud they encountered a huge V-shaped flock of geese honking their way through the sky. Jontu joined the V at one end and Norii joined at the other and they flew along with the geese honking and laughing.

As they left the geese Norii pointed down to a flock of sheep sleeping in the moonlight.

"No," said Jontu, "you wouldn't!"

"Come on, silly," replied Norii, "the sheep need the exercise!"

Adding action to words, Norii dived like a hawk toward the sheep with Jontu sputtering behind. At the last minute they pulled up over the startled sheep who scattered in several directions bleating as only disturbed sheep can.

Norii and Jontu laughed and laughed as they floated back among the clouds. They came to rest on a moonlit cloud which drifted over the sleeping countryside. There was no sound but that of the wind.

Norii looked at Jontu with merry eyes, "well, did I fulfill my promise? To come to you when you least expected me?"

"Most definitely! My dreams were never this much fun! Are you sure you're real?", asked Jontu and bit his lip immediately afterward.

Norii looked cross, "There you go again! I am as real as you are. Through your dreams you can see me, but if you keep wondering if I'm real, maybe I'll stop coming to visit."

It was at that moment that Jontu realized not only was Norii real but that she was coming to mean more to him by the moment.

"Please, I'm sorry - I don't know why I keep asking that. Well, that's not true either - I keep asking because you are like no one else in my life. Tell me more of your life".

"My life is a life of flying freely throughout this world. I have lived inside the night moon; I have seen wonders too many to be told. I have floated at the crest of a windy sand dune as a shining sunset sang a siren's song." And she sang in a soft, beautiful voice,

"Stay with me now just for a little while,

stay with me now until day is done.

Stay with me now just a little while longer,

for I will be gone until morning comes.

After a moments' pause, she continued, "I have ridden the cold winter wind across snow covered starlit prairies. I have shimmered like heat on a summer day as a small red-haired child fed ducks in a pond. I have ridden the ocean's great waves. And in all of this I have searched for someone to take away the loneliness by sharing all these wonders."

Norii fell silent with her head down. Hesitantly, Jontu reached out and stroked her hair. It shown and sparkled with stardust. The next moment they were holding each other with arms that were as real as anything else in the world.

As they looked in each other's eyes, unspoken words were shared; the meaning was clear.

"Norii, I . . . ", began Jontu as the sky began to brighten with the coming morning. Before he could finish the words, the rising sun caught him full in the face and he found himself falling from the clouds, falling away from Norii who held out her arms to him.

Falling, falling, and landing with a thud . . . on the floor in front of his armchair before the smoldering embers of the fire. Jontu looked around as anyone would from dreaming. Dreaming? Had it only been a dream? His soul ached more than his head where he had hit the floor.

"I kept asking her if she was real. I chose to believe that she was. But was it all a dream? Or is there reality in our dreams?"

Jontu picked himself up and held his head in his hands for a few moments. Then with a sigh he began to move into his day. It was baking day so soon the house was filled with scent of fresh dough followed by the delicious smells of baking bread.

When some of the villagers stopped by his house, they found Jontu

 in a melancholy state of mind and the bread he gave them! It was in the shape of clouds and geese and sheep and angels! They went away shaking their heads as they contemplated their odd-shaped bread.

After several days of walking around in a fog, Jontu decided that it was time for a road trip. Bidding his friends farewell, Jontu walked deep into the woods pausing from time to time to rest. Finally, he came to rest at the top of a steep hill that looked over a broad green valley. Here he found rest for his body and his soul.

He thought and pondered over his dream . . . or his reality . . . or . . . His mood ran from happy memories to gloomy wonderings and back. Finally, he just sat and let his gaze take in the beauty of the valley before him. The sun warmed him, and he began to feel sleepy when, just at that moment, a familiar shimmer appeared in the air around him.

"So here is where you've hidden," said Norii's laughing voice. "I've been looking for you all day! What are you doing up here?"

With relief that bordered on trembling, Jontu spoke, "Wishing I could fly, of course. But sadly, as a solid I'm stuck on this perch."

Norii's chuckle sent shimmers cascading through the air and her voice sent shimmers up and down Jontu's spine, "So you don't want to start the conversation with 'are you real'"?

His feelings for her rose to the surface as he answered, "Norii, you are more real to me than anything I could have ever hoped for. And my feelings for you have grown in the short time I've known you. But here, above this valley, all I can do is longingly wish you were real in my world."

And with this, tears rolled down Jontu's cheeks.

Her voice was soft and full of feeling and her presence caressed his cheek like a warm summer breeze, "I know, Jontu, I know. We are each real and we are each prisoner in our own world. My dear, what is to be done?"

"All that I know is that I will take any of you that life will allow, Norii, be it like this or in my dreams." replied Jontu.

"I must leave you now," Norii's voice said sadly, "I must return to the sky and rest. Come to me Jontu, come to me in your dreams." Her voice and shimmering-self floated freely upward.

Jontu sat until the sun slanted over the western sky. His deep feelings felt that they must burst skyward and join his love, but they did not know how. Finally, with a sigh too deep for words, Jontu arose and began the trek towards home. Never had he felt so hopeless and yet he could not give up hope.

While he was still several miles from his village, Jontu began to hear a noise in the distance that disturbed him. And even thought it was almost night, a flickering glow appeared in the trees above his path ahead.

As he hurried forward, he realized that something was on fire. Not something - a house fire! He rushed up to the wooden house. He knew the

family - a farmer, his wife, daughter and a new baby boy! Where were they? He called their names but there was no answer. He threw himself against the door - once, twice, a third time - and was rewarded with a splintering of wood as the door broke from it hinges.

Thick white smoke billowed from the open doorway. Taking a deep breath, he plunged into the opening. Staying low, he continued to call the names of the family. Suddenly he tripped over an obstacle - it was a leg. There he found the wife holding her baby covered with an old cloth. Carefully Jontu dragged them through the door and into the clear night air.

Taking only a moment to see that both were breathing, Jontu hurled himself again into the burning building. The smoke had given way to crackling flame and Jontu felt the heat of it on his skin. His clothing was smoldering as he found the father - the man was unconscious with burns on his face, but he also stilled breathed. Jontu shouldered the man and carried him outside as well.

The wife and baby were now crying and coughing. "Tend to your husband," shouted Jontu as he ran once more into the flames. Now he felt great pains in his arms and legs as the flames blocked his way. Still Jontu pushed on into the back room. Coughing great coughs, he felt his way over the floor until his burned hand encountered the little girl's hand.

Jontu picked her up and sheltered her in his arms, refusing to allow the flame to touch her further. The flames howled their anger and lashed out at Jontu, striking his face, his back, his legs and filling the air he breathed with smoke and flame.

Stumbling, half crawling, Jontu emerged that last time from the burning house. The roaring flames lept high into the surrounding trees and before he lapsed into unconsciousness, Jontu heard the shouts of the villagers as they came to offer help.

He awoke in his own bed but not in peace and comfort but in great wracking pain that roamed his body like a pack of wolves.

He tried to speak but only croaking sounds emerged followed by great pain. The old women of the village were at this side immediately, "shh, Jontu, shh - you must not try to speak. You are injured and must save your strength."

His eyes spoke questions that the women answered, "yes, Jontu, the family you saved are all well and sound. They suffered burns and from smoke, but they will all recover. Your courage has made you our hero all over again."

Jontu relapsed into unconsciousness. He drifted in and out of sleep.

He knew that he would not recover. During his wakeful periods, the family he saved came to see him. The women who tended him knew he had not long to live - his burns were too severe. He regained enough strength to speak in soft whispers and he shared with his friends in the village how to divide his earthly belongings.

One evening he awoke, and the sun shown in though the open window. He had dreamed again of Norii. The old woman sitting with Jontu was startled from a doze by a shimmering shower of color that appeared in the room over Jontu's bed. Her surprise became astonishment as a voice was heard in the room.

"Now we will be together always and forever, my Jontu, now we will become one, my love." The voice became silent. Jontu smiled through burned lips and whispered, "Norii . . .". Then his eyes closed, and his breathing stilled. The shimmer that was Norii was joined by a new shimmer in the air. The two entwined and danced as they rose through the window into the darkening skies.

And now, as real as real can be, Jontu and Norii are one forever.

The Clan rides the summer breezes from place to place. Sometimes they tell stories as they float through sunny skies.

6 THE KING OF CIRCUMSTANCES

Once there were six grumpy men. Their names were Alf and Lief and Ralph and Olaf and Lawrence and one that the rest called Stinky. When they were together their favorite pastime seemed to be complaining. If it was hot, they wished it were colder. If it was morning, they grumbled that nighttime was too long away. They grumbled about their lack of money and the poor condition of their clothing and shoes.

If food was abundant, they complained about being too full yet if food was scarce, they complained bitterly of hunger. They each had a gift for a particular type of complaining.

Alf could complain about the weather like no one else. His grumbling was a complete litany of weather-related ills.

Lief complained best about food. It was too hot or too cold or too spicy or too bland. Goldilocks and the bear's porridge was ambrosia compared to what Lief ate.

Ralph could grumble about people best of all. This person was too happy, this one too sad, the other too loud, and that person could not he heard no matter how he tried.

Olaf didn't like to work and knew the entirety of human ills. He was too tired to work or too sore or his lumbago was acting up or he had blisters.

Lawrence was best at grumbling about money. If he had any it was not enough, if he didn't have any, it was not to be borne.

And then there was Stinky. Stinky was the master. He could complain about any subject whether he knew anything about it or not. His favorite phrases often began with " . . . that's nothing. Let me tell you about the time . . ." and finished with another whopper of a complaint.

It finally came about that the five had had all of Stinky they could stand. One black night they shouldered their meager possessions and left - leaving Stinky snoring fitfully by himself. He awoke to the rumble of thunder and was about to try and bet Alf to complain about the weather when he saw that he was alone. Grumbling to himself (what else?) he looked for his companions; friends was too strong a word.

"What sort of sorry game is this?" he wondered. "I slept too poorly for this foolishness, and I am hungry as well. They will pay for their sport when I find them."

But the five were not to be found and for the first time in many years Stinky found himself alone. At first, he pretended that it did not matter, and he complained aloud to himself as he walked along. But as the hours stretched to days, Stinky began to be forlorn and his complaints gradually faded to silence.

As he sat by the side of the road wondering where he would find something to eat and feeling extremely sorry for himself, he was startled by a burst of happy song coming from around the bend in the road ahead. This merry melody maker was singing and whistling and almost shouting in happy abandon. The music makers' voice was deep and tuneful and Stinky was sure he was about to meet some nobleman or knight upon a gallant steed. He quickly stood up so he would not be stepped on and looked up to see what person could feel so full of joy.

But his eyes dropped, and his mouth fell open in astonishment as the singer came fully around the bend. No knight or nobleman this! A short bulbous shape clad in a jaunty arrangement of old clothes and rags came into sight. His huge mouth was open wide in song showing  mottled skin and wrinkles and folds which threatened to bury his over large and very unattractive nose.

He stopped dead on the road and roared in a voice that was four times bigger than his body, "Well met, my friend, I am overjoyed to find you. My name is Orren and I am of Gnomish extraction and I am on my way to a family reunion. How do you find yourself this happy day?"

Stinky's mouth closed and opened and closed again but nothing came out but some assorted guttural grunts.

Orren threw back his enormous head and laughed long and loud, "Caught you unawares, did I? Well, that happens. So how to you come to be here, my friend? What is your name and where are you bound? Tell me of your life and let me share the road with you."

Still amazed, Stinky managed to share the essentials of his current situation. "And so now I am left alone and forlorn with no friends and no prospects," Stinky finished. The problem was that without his old friends to echo his complaints, they felt a bit thin. Self-conscious now, Stinky looked foolishly down at his old shoes.

"Friendless?!" said Orren, "never, not as long as I share the road with you. Come and travel with me for a while, friend Stinky, and we'll see what wonders the world has for us today!"

"Wonders?", snorted Stinky, "The only thing I wonder is whether or not I'll get a meal today."

"I'll have a meal and it will be wonderful," said Orren. "I believe I'll have fried chicken with roasted potatoes and peas with some apple pie for good measure."

"And where," Stinky said with a swallow, "will you find this wonderful meal?"

"Where? I have no idea as yet, but it will come to me; just wait and see."

Stinky pondered this hopelessly. "He's going to get a meal, but he doesn't know where. He's happy for no reason that I can see. I wonder what I've gotten myself into here," thought Stinky as he edged nervously away from the happy gnome.

"Sir Gnome," said Stinky, "how can you be so sure you'll find a meal? Is there an Inn up ahead that you are aware of? I haven't eaten a decent meal in several days and I certainly don't have any money to buy a meal if we find one."

With a chuckle and a merry look, Orren replied, "Why you can have anything you want, my new friend. You only have to speak it and it will be so. Whatever I want I simply speak aloud, and it happens."

"What wonderful magic this is! How did you learn of it?", said Stinky. But before Orren could answer, Stinky smelled an odor that caused his empty belly to clench and rumble. It was the smell of chicken frying and the smell of fresh hot bread baking, and it was wonderful.

Stinky and Orren came over a small rise in the path and there before them was an amazing sight. A caravan of small horse drawn carts and wagons sat in the hollow before them. Around a blazing cook fire, a band of merry travelers sat eating and drinking and talking and laughing.

Walking among them, Orren and Stinky were welcomed with shouts. "Come, make yourself comfortable and eat with us, fellow travelers." said a small woman in a big hat.

Before they could think twice, they were eating golden fried chicken and roasted potatoes and peas and when they thought they could hold no more, the woman brought out a  freshly baked apple pie steaming with smells of apples and cinnamon.

After this wonderful meal, Stinky and Orren leaned back against a great oak tree. Stinky was so overwhelmed with the meal that he rapidly fell asleep; snoring and dreaming. And when he awoke the caravan was gone!

He shook Orren awake saying, "Sir Gnome, the caravan has vanished! Where have they gone?"

Orren sat up with an enormous jaw cracking yawn that threatened to envelop his head. With a stretch and a scratch Orren looked about him, "it matters not that they are gone - they fulfilled my wish and were on their way."

Stinky was confused still but the memory of such a wonderful meal the night before had improved his mood to the point that he forgot to complain! As Orren seemed to be preparing to continue his journey, Stinky asked if he could continue along with him.

"Of course, you may," the gnome boomed. "I would not have it any other way. Come, my friend, let us see what wonders the day holds for us."

As they walked together, Stinky was lost in thought. How could this gnome be so happy when he didn't know where his next meal would come from? How did he know that he would find exactly what he expected he would find? This Orren reacted exactly opposite to the way he would react to the same circumstances.

Orren contented himself with singing happy bits of song as they traveled along a sun-dappled path overhung with bright green tree branches. He sang:

"I say what I have" most folks' proclaim,

And since words come true,

they've no one to blame,

but themselves for their woes and their pain and their lack.

But "I have what I say" is what I proclaim.

And since words come true,

my words bring me fame,

And fortune and a heart that is merry.

So, I urge you today to consider your speech

And since words come true

your tongue you must teach

To speak only joy and wants all fulfilled

by the fruit of your tongue -

by the strength of your will.

Stinky wondered at the meaning of Orren's song. "Orren," he asked, "this song that you sing. Is it a child's nursery rhyme?"

Orren laughed aloud, "I assure you, my friend it is no nursery rhyme. It is the secret of life if you let it change your thinking."

"What can saying have to do with having? It certainly does not change things. Besides to say something contrary to what is real is to doubt your senses!"

The happy gnome looked at his companion, "If you believe that then you'll fulfill every bad thing you ever say. The law of saying works whether you believe it or not."

Before he could reply, Stinky felt a sudden gust of wind. Looking up he saw that the summer sky was filling with large gray clouds. Distant thunder rumbled and lightning flashed ahead of them.

"Ah, now we will be soaked for sure," grumbled Stinky. "This type of storm will leave us wet and cold - I have often seen it to be true."

Orren chuckled, "To be sure you will be wet and chilled. However, I believe I will pass on such discomfort. I'm sure that there will be a shelter up ahead that will protect me."

Walking quickly ahead, the gnome was soon out of sight around a bend in the path. Stinky simply stood there with a scowl on his face. "Humph. Foolish gnome - he'll be just as wet as I in a few minutes! 'Saying makes it so - Humph!'"

And in a few minutes, his words bore fruit and the sky opened up and poured down rain. It took only moments for Stinky to become thoroughly wet and miserable (which was often his state even when dry). As he trudged slowly up the road his only satisfaction was that Orren was just as wet as he and he looked forward to a hardy "I told you so".

His wry retort died on his lips a brief time later as he came across Orren smoking his pipe and as dry as could be seated under a rock outcropping next to the road. "Friend Stinky, come in out of the rain!", called the gnome. "Come under this shelter and begin to dry off!"

"How, why . . . .", Stinky began to stutter. "How do you manage to always get your way!? Here I am soaked to the skin and yet you avoided the rain. We were hungry and you came across food."

Orren didn't laugh, he only looked thoughtfully at Stinky. "I'm wondering if you are ready to hear my secret," the gnome said stroking his oversized nose with a finger. "I'm wondering if you are able to hear about what has become my way of life. Will you hear with an open mind? Will you reject what I have to say because it goes against common sense? Will you dismiss me because you have lived with the fruit of your beliefs for so long?"

Stinky sat quietly and considered the gnome's words. He had been unhappy so long that misery was a way of life for him. And though he complained long and loudly, in many ways misery and unhappiness had become what he was accustomed to. Did he even want to change?

With the passing of the storm, a bright ray of sunlight pierced the clouds, and, at the same time, something bright pierced his heart. And then the change came inside him - he *would* be different! He would change if it took him the rest of his life!

He turned to the silent gnome and said, "Friend Orren, your words have had a great effect on me. I look back at my life and am astounded at how much unhappiness I have invited, nay welcomed, into my life. I am ready to learn your magic. I am ready to take a new path no matter how strange it may be."

Orren paused before he spoke and considered his words. "A wise being once said that the words that we speak are like the rain falling. Rain falling from heaven is not simply water - but it is water that falls to the earth and waters it. The water sinking into the earth brings life to plants and animals. It accomplishes a purpose before rising again on the winds back into the heavens.

Our words are like drops of rain - they affect all the things around them. If we throw our words around carelessly, then we gather the bad fruit of careless words. If we choose the words we speak carefully, and realize that they accomplish what we say, then we reap a harvest of peace and happiness".

Stinky pondered this for a moment, "If, Sir Orren, this is true (and I have come to believe it is), then what have I done by to myself by taking on the name of rotting plants and garbage? How have my complaints and grumblings grown up if not as the sad circumstances of my life?" Tears welled up in his eyes as he continued, "If this is true then I have wasted so many years of my life, I have eaten the bitter fruit of careless words. How can I ever redeem my life? How can I change after so long sowing wrongful words?"

Orren looked on his friend with compassion, "Friend Stin...". He paused, "No I will no longer call you by that name for, from this time forward, you must begin a time of new planting. You must root up the weeds that have crowded out your good harvests. And you must begin by choosing a new name for yourself, a name that reflects the way you want to see yourself. For from this beginning will new, healthy fruit grow."

The sad man considered this for a moment. "Orren," he said, "more than anything else I want to be rich. I don't just mean rich in money or lands, but rich in life as I see you are. I want to bring happiness to others, to lift their load and to teach them that life and death are in the words that they choose to speak.

So, I now call myself Rich, the King of Circumstances, and that will be my name from here forward. And by that name may I come to be a blessing to those I encounter in my journey through life."

With this his face brightened and many of the old wrinkles caused by years of frowns began to fade. With a hearty laugh and a slap that threatened to dislocate his shoulder, Orren struck his new friend, Rich, with a friendly slap on the shoulders, "Now THERE'S a name to speak often and long and loud, King Rich!"

Soon afterward Rich and Orren parted ways with many mutual protestations of eternal friendship. Wherever he went now, when asked his name, his answer was, "I am Rich, King of Circumstances". And the words he planted not only overcame his old circumstances, they began to change his new life for the better. He learned to speak good about people and events and his past and his present and especially his future. Throughout the rest of his life, whenever he would meet with others along the road of life, they invariably came away happier for having met him.

One bright summer day, as he traveled toward a meeting with his friend Orren, Rich encountered five men seated by the side of the road. "Hail and good morning," he shouted at them as he approached.

"What's so good about it," said one man, "The day is hot already and the sun will be a tiresome companion today."

"Yes, " said the next, "and I have not eaten in two days; even then it was cold and clotted and not fit for human consumption."

"You all sicken me," said the third, "I cannot for the life of me figure out why I stay with such low life companions as you."

"I am too tired and sore to listen to this drivel," said the fourth, "We would be happier if we had not had to work for that farmer yesterday. I am exhausted."

"Yes, and even then, we got only half the money we were promised by that stingy farmer," said the fifth, "how was I to know he wanted a full days' work?"

For Rich had indeed found his old "friends", though that word now seemed very strange in his mind. As they looked at him with a mixture of displeasure and impatience, one of them paused.

Alf said, "Do we know you? There is something about you that seems familiar - but the sun is in my eyes, and I may be mistaken."

Leif and Ralph and Olaf and Lawrence stared at Rich but finally decided that they were mistaken. They knew no one with such a bright, happy, hopeful countenance.

And as for Rich, well, what do you think he did for his old "friends"?

Earth Stories

Little Tet was crying fretfully. "I want something to eat and I'm tired of waiting for it!" PIng flew over with a bite of honey the size of a dew drop. He began to tell little Tet this story so he would understand the problems that are caused by impatience.

7 THE IMPATIENT FARMER

There once was an impatient farmer. How he ever became a farmer is a story itself. But needless to say, he was impatient. When it was winter, he longed for spring. When it was spring, he talked only about summer. When everyone was enjoying long summer days, he complained that it was not yet autumn. And when autumn brought the harvest and cooler days, he said that he had always looked forward to winter.

The man, whose name was Frilato, inherited the farm from his uncle who had been a very successful and prosperous farmer. Frilato came to the farm in early autumn and found an abundant harvest of wheat and apples and corn.

His neighbors felt sorry for Frilato because he knew nothing about farming. Several of them came to the farmhouse to talk with him. "Frilato", they said, "your uncle was a great farmer. The harvest you see is the result of his experience and skill and patience. Let us help you with your harvest so you can learn how it is done."

Now Frilato knew better than to look a gift horse in the mouth (having once been bitten by a horse when he was a small child) but he was also impatient. "All right, all right", he said, "let's begin. I must learn all I can as quickly as I can."

As they began, his neighbors showed Frilato how to select the best apples, and the richest sheaves of wheat and the fullest and brightest ears of corn for seed for the next year. The seed apples and wheat and

corn they stored in special areas of the barn so that it would be safe until spring.

Frilato was a good enough person to remember to thank his neighbors for all their help. But then his impatience began to cause problems. He sold his crops in the market but didn't keep enough on hand to feed himself and his animals throughout the long dark winter. The money he got for the crops he used to buy additional oxen so he could plough the fields more quickly when spring came.

As autumn skies gave way to snow clouds, Frilato became more and more impatient. He could hardly wait until spring so he could plant and look forward to another harvest. He fed his animals from the rapidly dwindling stocks of grain he had saved, and, by late winter, he was facing shortages for himself and his animals.

One cold winter night, as he sat and worried about what to do, (impatiently, of course) there came a knock at his door. "Who could that be at this hour and in this cold?" wondered Frilato. As he opened the door, the wind whipped around a stooped shape standing there. "Well, don't just stand there, come in, come in," cried Frilato.

The shape was wrapped all in coats and shawls and scarves against the cold. A voice came from some undetermined place from within the mass of cloth, "Why, thank you, Frilato, I believe I will come in and have a warm." Moving with no particular haste, the cloth-wrapped shape came into the warm bright kitchen. Shifting itself towards the fireplace, the shape began slowly to unwrap and unbutton and unwind until the bright face of an old man was seen in the reflection of the flickering flames. Firelight made the old man's eyes sparkle like stars on a clear summer night.

The old man regarded Frilato kindly. Frilato frankly stared. "Who are you, my good sir, and how do you know my name?" Frilato was impatient to know who this stranger was.

"I am called Pattrio, and I own a farm in the next valley. I was your uncle's friend and it is only now that I have been able to pay my respects."

Frilato was astounded, "But, sir, my uncle died last winter just after the new year. How is it that it has taken you so long to come?" Then remembering his manners, Frilato pulled another chair near the hearth.

"Patience, Frilato, patience," said the old man. Frilato kept the thought to himself that patience was not one of his virtues. "I have come to pay my respects to my friend, your uncle, by helping his nephew learn to farm."

"Pattrio, I have spent almost a year now seeking knowledge of how to farm. Through these dark months I have had much time to reflect, and it seems to me that I am not made to be a farmer. Things seem to move so slowly, and I seem to be unable to adjust myself to the slow pace of farming."

Pattrio smiled slowly; in fact, everything the old man did seemed as slow moving as the winter months before spring arrives, "You do need knowledge of farming but beyond that you need wisdom. Wisdom is taking in knowledge and allowing it to age slowly and carefully like fine wine. Your neighbors provided knowledge throughout the late summer and autumn. Now during these winter months knowledge can become wisdom. If you allow wisdom to have its' full effect, then you will succeed in your farming."

Less impatiently now, Frilato asked, "But HOW does knowledge become wisdom? What can I do to learn wisdom? So far I have failed miserably."

Pattrio reached into his tattered bag, "I have brought you a teacher of wisdom. Wisdom comes through contemplation and patience, and I have brought you someone who has learned both." His hands removed a small shape which Frilato was surprised to see move! It was a small bird which Pattrio placed on the kitchen table.

"I will leave my friend here with you, Frilato, and if you will patiently consider his ways, I promise you will learn wisdom - and through wisdom come to contentment. For lack of contentment is the root of all your impatience and unhappiness. And with that, Pattrio wrapped his clothing around himself and with a slow wave, slipped away into the cold and blowing night.

The bird was small and handsome, his sleek brown and tan back a sharp contrast to his yellow breast. But like the stately old gentleman who had left him he walked with a slight hobble from a deformed right foot. And that, perhaps, was his best trait, for it showed the uncommon courage and perseverance of his spirit as he dealt with Mother Nature for life and the right to live out his days in search of food.

Mother Nature has a sharp kindness bordering on the cruel, it seemed to Frilato, and the bird had survived her harsh judgement on the weak and deformed long enough to grow to adulthood. As Frilato watched the bird limp about in the snow foraging for food, he felt a twinge of guilt as he thought of the times he had complained of lost opportunity or the unfair lot in life he had drawn.

He began to see that patience came along with contentment - or at least acceptance - of where we are in life. He saw that, just as the Crippled Bird's only hope was patiently working to find food, the farmer's only hope is in the patient waiting for the harvest after the planting of seed.

For before him was one of God's creatures that had asked for only the chance to live and search for its daily bread, while he, Frilato, in the midst of plenty had cried bitter tears because he was not served Life from a golden bowl.

Small signs of spring brought changes to winter's fare. The sun rose a little earlier and, here and there, the rich brown of the fields began to poke through the snow. By a changed attitude and some hard work and the help of his friend, the crippled bird, Frilato had managed to feed himself and his animals and save just enough seed to plant his fields.

On the day he went forth to begin to plow the newly thawed earth, Frilato saw the Crippled Bird take wing and fly away and Frilato's spirit flew with him to the reaches of heaven where he thanked his Creator for the precious life he had been given.

Frilato then and there asked that he might live his life as did the small sleek bird with his deformed leg - with patience and courage and contentment and without complaint.

8 THE STILLNESS BROKEN

The day was bright blue and hot; the temperature crawled lazily upward on a summer afternoon. The small town was still; even the dust in the streets had settled. Everyone who could be inside was inside with the shutters closed rocking in the parlor and fanning themselves with last week's edition of the Post or sitting in the kitchen swatting flies that landed on the table. Even the blacksmith sat under a tree and whittled, waiting for the cool of the evening.

In the midst of the stillness a small sound intruded. A sleepy old horse stirred his drooping ears to listen as he stood at the hitching post. The merchant at his dry goods paused in his counting to listen.

The sound, though far away, was high pitched and shrill. It floated into the small town and then back out again, past the old schoolhouse which was shuttered for the summer and then into the bright green of the deep woods beyond.

It was cooler here where the thick branches dappled the floor of the forest with patterns of sunlight. The excited sound grew louder and seemed to wend along a rough path through the heart of the forest. A bright-eyed squirrel paused on a branch to listen and then silently disappeared into the leaves. An old box turtle sat on a warm rock and blinked at the sound.

The path sloped gently downward through a small open glen filled with fragrant grasses where a startled rabbit bounded for home and safety. It was now possible to distinguish the excited shouting of laughter and play. But how could such excitement exist on such a still hot quiet day?

Turning through several more trees, the path breasted a small rise just barely in time to see a small, sunburned, blond-haired shape fling himself onto a thick hanging vine, swing out into the air, and disappear, happily shrieking into the old swimming hole!

Boys of assorted shapes and sizes were engaged in merrily diving, dunking, and in general, being as wet as they possibly could. The water was cool from early summer rains and the great old trees shaded the banks and the boys ran down the hill to catch the swing vine, propelling themselves out over the sun-streaked water. Each tried to outdo the next in the size of splash produced. Oh, how wonderful to be cool and wet and free on this hot still summer day!

The boys' antics continued throughout the long summer afternoon 'til the rays of sunshine began to slant more and more from the west. An early evening breeze sprang up, breaking the stillness and causing the leaves to murmur sleepily as they woke from their nap.

One by one, the boys gradually climbed from the water, shaking themselves to dry. They collected their clothes from this branch and that bush and slowly dressed themselves.

The evening had begun, and it was time for them to head home for their suppers. With many a backward glance and sigh, the boys started up the path toward home.

The broken stillness returned - for a time.

The shadows have lengthened, and night is fast approaching. Gathering their belongings, the Shadow Clan prepares to move on. With many a sigh and backward glance, they take to the night air to seek a place of rest.

Tomorrow they will again go forth to hear stories and to make mischief and to hide in the midst of the shadows that they call home.

ABOUT THE AUTHOR

Hal Warfield writes technical documentation for a global data company. Hal has written additional books on technical subjects, but Shadow Clan is his first children's book.

Made in the USA
Columbia, SC
19 December 2023

29052752R00065